Where Would We Be
Without Him/Her?

ORLA
KELLY
PUBLISHING

Jimmy Dunne

Orla Kelly Publishing
27 Kilbrody,
Mount Oval,
Rochestown,
Cork,
Ireland.

All the characters in this book are fictitious and any resemblance to actual persons, living or dead is purely coincidental.

This book is dedicated to my wife Marian (The love of my life)

About the Author

A child of the fifties, James (Jimmy) Dunne grew up in Phibsboro Dublin 7 Ireland. He vividly remembers the Drovers herding their cattle up North Circular Road to the market for slaughter.

At the age of 16 years, he enlisted in the Irish Defence Forces and served 24 years. Most of that time in Collins Barracks Dublin 8, now a National Museum.

He is a member of The Irish United Nations Veterans Association (I.U.N.V.A.) having served two tours of peacekeeping duty in Southern Lebanon (UNIFIL). He is also a member of The National Ex-Service Personnel (O.N.E.) Oglaigh Naisiunta na hEireann.

A Dunboyne resident Co. Meath Ireland, he is now enjoying his retirement.

Contents

About the Author   v

Chapter 01   1

Chapter 02   4

Chapter 03   7

Chapter 04   10

Chapter 05   14

Chapter 06   17

Chapter 07   20

Chapter 08   25

Chapter 09   29

Chapter 10   33

Chapter 11   39

Chapter 12   44

Chapter 13   49

Chapter 14   53

Chapter 15   58

Chapter 16   62

Chapter 17   67

Chapter 18   71

Chapter 19   76

Chapter 20   80

Chapter 21   83

Chapter 22	86
Chapter 23	91
Chapter 24	95
Chapter 25	100
Chapter 26	104
Chapter 27	108
Chapter 28	111
Chapter 29	114
Chapter 30	118
Chapter 31	121
Chapter 32	127
Chapter 33	129
Chapter 34	132
Chapter 35	136
Chapter 36	139
Chapter 37	143
Chapter 38	145
Chapter 39	148
Chapter 40	150
Chapter 41	153
Chapter 42	157
Chapter 43	161
Acknowledgements	163
Please Review	165

01

"OH MY GOD, Sheila. Are you alright? Are you hurt? Do you need money? What are you going to do?"

"Stop Joe, stop, for God's sake. Will you just listen to me for one second? I'm fine, honestly".

"I feel like such a fool", as Sheila tried to explain, "I got off the bus and found myself a baggage trolley, not thinking I put my handbag into the basket while I fixed my cases onto the trolley. I didn't notice a thing until I heard Joan shouting and running towards me. When I looked up, I saw a man running to a waiting motorbike with my handbag. There was nothing I could do. It was over in seconds as I watched them speed away. Look Joe, honestly, I'm fine; Joan got in a tizzy when it happened, but I told her the same as you. I also told her to go home without me as I am not afraid being alone. Joe, it is a beautiful island and I feel safe here, so don't worry; I know what you are like. Look I'm ringing you from a call phone and I haven't much change. I'm just saying not to meet the plane tonight as I won't be on it. My passport, phone, and tickets were in the bag, but luckily they didn't get my purse with my money or credit cards as I had them in my pocket. Security is with me at the moment; they said I will have to report the theft at the police station back in the resort. I will also have to apply for an emergency passport so I can return home. It's going to take a few days to get these, but please don't worry. I will return to the hotel where I stayed in Los Christianos and book in again for an extra few nights. When everything is sorted, I'll let you know what flight I've arranged to come home on". Joe seemed to be appeased but before he hung up, he wanted to be reassured and asked her one more time...

"Sheila, are you sure you are OK?"

"Absolutely Joe, now try not to worry". As Sheila hung up the phone, she could feel the trickle of sweat roll down her face and her blouse stick to the small of her back as lying to her best friend Joe was not in her nature. But this was not a normal situation; if he found out, he would be so hurt and offended with her to know that she had broken her promise.

For the moment, all she could think about was returning to her hotel and re-booking some more time there to see if the person she had seen was truly him. It was only a chance sighting and she couldn't be sure, but she knew if she had got on that flight home, she would regret it for the rest of her life. This was her last chance to put her mind at rest and not to take it would be madness.

All that Joe knew was, she was going on a week's sun holiday with her friend from work; just a bit of relaxation and fun as Joe didn't like to fly, and he didn't even possess a passport. He said the break would do her good, and he would look after the house while she was gone, so as he said, "It will work out fine".

Sheila felt so guilty knowing she was still in Tenerife, but if things didn't work out, Joe or Rose would never have to know. On the day she was leaving Tenerife, the bus journey out to the airport from Playa Las Americas went too fast as she had so much to think about. What if she was wrong? What if she was mistaken? What would happen if it was him? How would she confront him? Did she just imagine it was him? Or, was she losing her mind? What excuse would she give Joe if she stayed in Tenerife longer?

She had already arrived at the airport; her mind was still racing, and her story was concocted. She hoped Joe believed her. Now that she was seated on the bus back to her hotel, she checked her handbag and took out her mobile phone to switch it off. She put it back in her bag beside her passport. With the beautiful evening sunset on her face, she looked out the window and looked up at snow-capped volcanic Mount Teide, the highest mountain in Spain, and her mind began to wander back to when this whole sorry story began. The six years it took to arrive here on this bus now, where she was still searching for him and still hoping he was alive, knowing that on the seventh year he would be declared legally dead and she would become homeless.

02

When Joe hung up, he thought for a moment before deciding to ring Rose as he was worried sick. He told her what Sheila had said about her passport being stolen at the airport and how he didn't really believe her story. He also said that he feared Sheila was having a relapse of the episode she had four years ago in Cyprus. Rose listened intently to what Joe had to say before bellowing...

"That fucking bitch is only looking for notice, and it's all because dad has been missing six years and I said I wanted the house sold. The proceeds of the sale would be split evenly between the two of us after the seventh year when he was declared dead. Well, she can pull all the fucking stunts she fucking wants, but I'm not changing my mind; I want my share and that's it. That fucking breakdown in Cyprus cost me a fortune with doctor's fees and counselling, not to mention the cost of changing flights and the extra accommodation. If she thinks I'm doing it again, she has another thing coming".

When Rose had finished her rant, Joe cut in timidly, "But Rose, she's your only sister and you can't leave her in Tenerife all alone; God knows what could happen to her".

Rose shouted back at Joe even louder, "She's over twenty-one and well able to look after herself. She has to realise there are consequences to her actions and I'm not my sister's keeper".

Joe getting worried cut in again saying, "But Rose, what are we going to do?"

"What do you mean, WE?" Rose replied... "You are only her fucking friend and neighbour and you have no say in what goes on in our family, so keep your fucking nose out of our business", Rose continued. "When Sheila runs out of money and realises nobody is coming to save her this time, she will come home quick enough. She will also find that nothing has changed. That house will be sold and that will be the end to it". Rose hung up.

After cutting off Joe, Rose tossed her phone across the table in temper while shouting, "That fucking bitch".

Her husband Frank raised his head from reading his paper and asked the question, "Trouble love?" Rose ranted on and on about her sister Sheila playing her fucking stupid games in Tenerife and how she was not going to get away with it. Frank continued to look concerned and interested while keeping one eye on what he was reading, because Frank knew only too well not to interrupt Rose when she was in one of her tempers.

Of course Frank had no interest in Rose's tirade; he didn't care about that little two up, two down terraced yellow and red brick town house on Oxmanstown road, Stoneybatter, Dublin 7. Frank would never say it to

Rose, but he couldn't understand why she wanted the little house sold in the first place making her only sister homeless. He knew when the sale went through and the proceeds were split between them, there would be little enough left for Sheila to buy a property. House prices had gone up drastically in the north Dublin city centre area in the last few years.

Sheila was a decent soul and Frank felt really sorry for the situation that Rose was putting her sister in, but that was her family home and her own business. Frank knew better not to intervene as life for him would be made unbearable; he also knew when Rose had finished her rant and cooled off, life would return to normal. They lived in their five bedroom detached home in the affluent area of Castleknock Dublin 15 with a double garage, which housed their two Mercedes. They also had membership of Castleknock golf and country club, so for a quiet life, what was best for Frank was to keep his mouth shut for now.

03

F rank didn't know what Rose was going on about saying how much she had spent when Sheila had her breakdown in Cyprus, because it was he who had funded that trip as Rose hadn't worked from the day they were married ten years previously. Frank worked as a sales executive in the Irish Financial Services centre. Rose worked as a waitress in a trendy gastro pub where he would have lunch or occasionally drop into the pub after work for a few wind-down drinks. He always found Rose attentive and friendly; she was a very attractive girl with long black hair and a tidy figure.

It was around Christmas time and being the busiest time for the end of the year accounts, Frank was working all day with no time for lunch. As it was also the break up day before the festivities began, he wanted to clear his desk and take a few well-earned days off. When he had finished, tired and hungry, he decided to head to the gastro pub for a well-earned drink and something to eat. When Frank opened the door of the pub, it was absolutely heaving with people enjoying the Christmas spirit. Smiling and enjoying the atmosphere, he pushed his way to the bar to get a drink and order some food, but the bar staff were so busy it took a while before he could even get their attention.

Eventually he caught the eye of Sean the barman and ordered a pint of Guinness and a sandwich. Over the noise and shouting, Sean apologised saying the kitchen had closed as they had run out of food since seven pm. Frank, feeling the pangs of hunger in his stomach, looked at his watch and was surprised to see it was past eight pm. As Sean put his pint on the counter, Frank asked was there anything at all left over in the kitchen as he hadn't eaten anything all day? Sean feeling a little sorry for his regular customer said to leave it with him and he would see what he could do.

While he sat at the counter feeling hungry and a little sorry for himself thinking he should have finished work earlier to join in the Christmas festivities, Rose tapped him on the shoulder. Smiling and shouting as best she could over the noise, she told him there was nothing left in the kitchen except some heels of bread but if he wanted, she would make him a sandwich of leftovers. Frank accepted gratefully so Rose fought her way to the kitchen to prepare him something to eat. Frank, relieved sat back on the bar stool to enjoy his first pint of the day and join in the Christmas spirit.

After a while, Rose returned with a most amazing sandwich between two heels of bread full of turkey and ham with stuffing, chips, and a salad dressing on the side.

The guy sitting next to him looked on in envy saying, "Wow, it looks like Santa came early for you".

Frank relished every bite of his sandwich and enjoyed the fact that he had gotten VIP treatment while his fellow revellers looked on with their mouths watering. When he had finished eating, he intended to pay for his food immediately as he knew the catering staff would be going home as soon as they had cleaned up. He wanted to leave a big tip for the excellent service he had received so he called Rose to pay for his food bill. Rose waved him away saying she couldn't charge him for leftovers while wishing him a very happy Christmas as she went about her business of clearing any last tables before her shift ended. Frank was really grateful and offered her twenty euro tip for looking after him saying that she had been a lifesaver.

Rose smiling took the tip saying it was her pleasure and carried on cleaning as Frank thought to himself, "Should I ask her out for a drink?" But by the time he had thought of it, Rose had already turned away and continued to clear the last few tables, so Frank went back to his stool and ordered another pint.

04

Later that night and after a few more pints, Frank decided to call it a day and head home; he had a nice modern apartment in Spencer dock overlooking the river liffey. It was a short walk, about three hundred meters from the pub; he was happy living there as it was handy for his work and he had all the facilities of the city centre on his doorstep. As he walked, he thought to himself, tomorrow he would do a little Christmas shopping around town then make arrangements to spend Christmas at home with his parents who lived in Dunboyne Co Meath where he grew up. As he exited the pub, the streets were thronged with revellers, some wearing red and white Santa hats holding a drink in their hands, laughing and singing. When he reached the corner to crossover the Samuel Beckett Bridge, he saw Rose standing at a kerb; two guys obviously with too much drink on them were making a nuisance of themselves and Rose didn't look comfortable with the attention they were giving her.

Frank approached her, putting his arm around Rose's shoulder asking, "Is everything ok here, love?" while eyeing the two guys at the same time.

Rose looked up at Frank with relief saying.

"Yes darling, these two gentlemen were just leaving".

When the men eyed up Frank's height and biceps, they decided it might be easier to move on and have some fun elsewhere. When the men had moved on, Frank removed his arm from Rose's shoulder as she explained that she was frantically trying to wave down a taxi for the last hour since leaving work. Frank noticed that she was shivering and chilled to the bone from the icy December wind blowing up the river liffey. So raising both hands in surrender, he said... "Look, don't take this the wrong way, or read anything into this, but I live just across the river from here", while pointing at his apartment block. "If you want, you can come up and get yourself warmed up. Afterwards, when the streets quieten down a bit, you can call a taxi from my place to take you home".

Rose smiled at Frank agreeing that it might be a good idea. As they both entered the apartment, Rose whistled, exclaiming it was a very nice place as she looked around. Frank was glad the cleaner had been in during the day as his bachelor pad could look a real mess after he had left for work. As he switched on the coffee machine, he offered her a cup; he knew there was no food in the place as he ate out most of the time. He was surprised when Rose asked if he had anything stronger. Happy to show off, Frank opened up his fancy art deco drinks cabinet with all the bottles and glasses displayed in front of a lighted mirror. Rose, looking really impressed, said she would love a gin and tonic; so Frank delighted with the way things were progressing poured two gin and tonics, then clinking their glasses together, they wished each other a happy Christmas. As Frank put on some music, Rose made herself comfortable on the white Italian leather sofa with her drink.

It was early in the morning when Frank awoke; it took him a few minutes to focus as he had a blinding headache. As he looked around the bedroom, he saw Rose lying naked beside him as he was. He tried to remember what happened the night before, but all he could remember was they drank, danced, and laughed. As he looked at Rose lying beside him, he tried to figure out the sequence of events that led to her sleeping in his bed and how did they end up naked? He then began to have flashbacks and asked himself the question, am I imagining it or did she make the first move and kiss me? Then Rose woke and turned over to smile at him; Frank was not sure what to say and smiled back as she exclaimed, "Wow that was some night".

She moved closer and put her head in the crook of his arm. As Frank felt her breast softly touching his side, he also felt her hand sliding across under the sheets caressing him and immediately he became aroused. So Frank thought, what's a guy to do? But just go with it and enjoy the moment with this beautiful woman who wanted him now.

Frank never went out for Christmas shopping that day; in fact, he never went home to his parents for a family Christmas get-together. He and Rose stayed in his apartment sending out for takeaways while shacking up together. That was eleven years ago now as they were married the following year and the time had gone by in a flash.

05

The next day, feeling very concerned for Sheila and still reeling from Rose's outburst, Joe waited outside Tommy O'Gara's pub in Stonybatter where she worked as a bar person since losing her job in the Shelbourne Hotel. She had worked in the hotel as a silver service waitress with her dad casually catering for weddings and conferences etc. Joe never really quite knew why she lost her job and Sheila never confided in him about what had happened. It must have been pretty bad as she said she never ever wanted to talk about it and Joe being her friend, would never push her to know why.

As soon as Joan, her work colleague who she travelled to Tenerife with her arrived for work, Joe approached her asking what had happened in Tenerife that she would leave Sheila there on her own. Joan, totally bewildered and knowing Joe and Sheila were good friends and neighbours said that she couldn't tell him anything. As she tried to explain, she said that one minute they were in the departure area queueing at the check-in desk when Sheila turned and apologised to Joan saying she would not be travelling home with her as there was something she had to check out before she left Tenerife. She told Joan she would follow her in a few days. Also, would she explain to Tommy their manager that she needed a few more days off work? With that she kissed and hugged her telling her not to worry before walking out of the terminal.

Joan continued with tears in her eyes. "I didn't know what to do, whether to follow her out of the terminal, or board the flight".

But as her husband would be waiting for her in Dublin and she felt Sheila knew what she was doing, she decided to return home and hoped Sheila would be in touch soon.

Joe's fears were confirmed; he knew the story Sheila had told him about her bag being stolen was false but what could he do now? All he could think about was poor Sheila over in Tenerife in God knows what state and on her own. He couldn't phone Rose, for he knew that she would tell him off for interfering in their family business. And anyway, he hated the way she had spoken to him saying, he had nothing to do with their family, when somehow he felt that he was always part of their family.

Joe grew up next door to the Callerys and from the time Joe, Sheila, and Rose were toddlers, they would play, eat, and sometimes sleep together between both houses. There was never a cross word spoken between Mr and Mrs Callery and his mum and dad, who were more elderly and Joe was their only child. Whenever there were birthday parties or any festivities, he would always be included or they were in their house for his. Rose would always play with her dolls and liked dressing them up using make up and girly things, while Sheila was more of a tomboy who liked the rough and tumble of playing football with boys. Joe, a little quieter and older than Sheila felt he was her protector, but if the truth be known, it was Sheila who protected him. Joe wasn't very physical, and when there was fighting to be done, as kids do fight, it was Sheila who would wade in to protect Joe. So when Sheila was around, nobody messed with Joe and Joe loved her for that, and still loved her to this day.

He knew that if Sheila would have him, he would marry her in a heartbeat and would live happily ever after, but he also knew their friendship would never lead to marriage and Joe would never jeopardise their friendship of over 30 years by asking her to marry him. Joe remembered when both his parents passed away within months of each other; it was Sheila who stood by their graveside hugging him while he wept. He also remembered it was Mr & Mrs Callery who helped him arrange both their funerals and hosted the receptions afterwards in their own home.

06

Joe was in his mid-thirties, of medium build, slightly balding with a comb over and dressed in black corduroy trousers, white shirt and gray cardigan. He had an unhealthy pallor from working nightshifts and a shy demeanour. He lived alone now and was very happy to have Sheila call on him regularly for a cup of tea and a chat or an evening meal while they listened to music. Joe and Rose didn't share the same friendship; she was more of a girls' girl and would taunt Joe as a child saying, "he was a Nancy boy", which would make Joe cry and made her laugh all the more at him while she stuck out her tongue.

Joe was glad when Rose married Frank, though he did get an invitation to the wedding as Sheila's plus one. Joe couldn't have been more proud to be seen linked with Sheila as they marched down the aisle after the wedding. Although Joe did have to sit at another table as Sheila was the chief bridesmaid sitting beside Rose at the top table, he didn't mind in the least. It must have been one of the biggest weddings ever held on Oxmanstown Road, Stonybatter. They were married in The Church of the Sacred

Heart, which was a Military church behind Collins Barracks in Arbour Hill. The length of the stretch limousine alone found it hard to turn into the church grounds, and the plush wedding reception was held in the Castleknock Golf and Country club where Frank was a member.

Rose was indeed a beautiful bride, but Joe's eyes never left Sheila who looked stunning, if not a little uncomfortable all dressed up in a bridesmaid dress. Normally she would be dressed in a black aviator jacket, black T shirt, with a studded leather watchstrap, black ankle length jeans and maroon bovver boots; her black hair would be cropped into a shoulder length bob. He remembered looking up at her during the long after dinner speeches while catching her eye and winking at her; then she gave him the biggest smile back. Joe thought his heart would burst because, to him Sheila Callery was the most beautiful girl there.

Rose being the complete opposite to Sheila would always appear immaculately dressed in designer clothes she liked to accessorise in natural tones, with manicured nails, professional makeup, the latest Louis Vuitton handbag, gold Rolex watch, and wearing Jimmy Choo stilettos. Frank was a tall dark man about town who wore an Armani suit, white silk shirt and tie, manicured nails, well cut hair, Louis Vuitton brown leather shoes, and sporting a Tag Heuer watch. After they returned from their honeymoon in the Caribbean, Frank and Rose bought a big house together in Castleknock and Joe was glad, because his friendship with Sheila continued to grow stronger. But now with this awful situation in Tenerife, Joe was sick with worry. As he paced the floor, he wondered how he could help her. Joe didn't know what to do, his mind was racing, and he thought to himself. "Could I fly over to Tenerife and save her?"

But then he thought, "I am only a night security man in Grangegorman student campus; I do have some savings put by for a rainy day, and this is certainly a rainy day, but I have never travelled abroad before. In fact, I don't even possess a passport. The furthest I have ever been from home was when I brought my parents for a day out to Galway in the car". As far as Joe knew, Tenerife was in Spain, but it was a big country and he didn't know which part she was in. Joe didn't know that Tenerife was a tropical island in the middle of the Atlantic Ocean off the west coast of Africa.

07

He began to think back when all this trouble had started for Sheila; it was eight years earlier when her mother died suddenly of a massive stroke. Her father Neil was still serving overseas in Cyprus as a cook sergeant with the United Nations; he had to cut his trip short and come home to lay his wife to rest. Joe felt very sorry for the whole family and it was his turn to support Sheila as she wept standing beside her mother's grave. Poor Mr Callery was distraught as they lowered his wife's coffin into the earth. After the funeral, they went back to Castleknock golf and country club for refreshments so Joe accompanied Sheila. Rose arranged the whole funeral while Mr Callery travelled home from Cyprus, and as Rose had arranged everything, it was a big fancy affair with Rose at the forefront directing catering staff to do this and that when obviously it would have been done already. Joe knew that this was not the type of funeral Mr Callery would have wanted as he would have preferred a more low key reception, but the poor man was so devastated that he just let Rose take over as he sat quietly in the background.

After the funeral, Neil Callery never returned to Cyprus to finish his tour of duty; he just seemed to withdraw more and more into himself. Joe would call on him from time to time and invite him down for a pint in Tommy O Gara's pub while Sheila was working just to get him out of the house.

One evening, while sitting at the bar, Neil turned to Joe and gave him a great compliment; he told Joe he was more like a son to him than a neighbour. He said that Joe was a great support to his whole family during the sad passing of his beloved wife Mary, and it was a comfort to know he was around to keep an eye on Sheila should anything ever happen to him. Joe was chuffed at the compliment and beamed a big smile at Neil saying he was glad to be there and always would be for Sheila or indeed himself if ever they needed him. Later on, Joe couldn't put his finger on it, but he felt a little uncomfortable at Neil's statement while they sat quietly drinking their pints and enjoying each other's company.

As time passed, Neil withdrew even more into himself; when Joe would call to ask him out for a drink, he wouldn't answer the door. Although the house lights were off and it seemed the house was empty, Joe would have heard the front door close if he had gone out. When Joe met him afterwards and mentioned he had called to see him, Neil would say he was down in Collins Barracks NCO's mess meeting with some of his army mates.

It was later that Sheila confided in Joe that she was at her wits' end worrying about her father as she found out he had retired from the army six months previously and had said nothing. She continued that the army was his life and she didn't know what he was going to do with himself now. After Sheila confronted Neil about it, he just shrugged his shoulders saying he would find something, but what worried her most was that he said that if he hadn't been away on duty in Cyprus when Mary had her stroke, maybe she wouldn't have died. Sheila refuted the statement saying that nobody could have saved her mother as it was a massive stroke, which meant she would have been dead before any help would have arrived, but that didn't seem to reassure her father.

Sheila still worried about her father, decided to contact Rose telling her that Neil was still very melancholy and about the fact that he had retired from the army without discussing it with anyone. Rose was very blasé about her worries saying that he would be fine as he needed more time to get over her mother's death and find his way, then she said... "Anyway, if he needed some work, I can give him something to do in the garden as I am not happy with my present gardener".

But shortly after this, for some unknown reason, Rose did come to the house during the day when Sheila was out at work.

Joe was resting off his night shift that morning when he was awoken by Rose shouting and cursing at Neil; he could hear everything through the thin walls next door. He could hear that Neil was speaking normally and didn't seem to retaliate at her ranting. After about what seemed like an hour of this onslaught of abuse, Rose left the house in a temper while slamming the front door as hard as she could and driving away in her Mercedes with a screech of tyres. A while later, when Joe was still lying in bed and trying to go back asleep; he wasn't quite sure, but as he listened intently, he thought he could hear the sound of Neil crying.

Joe, very worried at this stage couldn't settle, so he got up and went next door to see if Neil was alright. After knocking on the door for about fifteen minutes and getting no answer, he decided to go down to Tommy O 'Gara's pub to tell Sheila what he had heard. Sheila, having listened to Joe's tale, thought about it for a while, then she said that Rose, in her own ham fisted way was probably trying to shake her dad up and hopefully take him out of himself. She also reassured Joe that when she had finished her shift, she would go straight home to see if Neil was ok and keep an eye on his behaviour.

When Sheila got home that evening and not letting on that she knew anything had happened earlier, she asked her dad if there was any news. She put on the kettle while watching him from the corner of her eye. Neil smiling, replied that Rose had called in during the day but had nothing strange to tell her as she didn't stay very long. Unperturbed, Neil just continued watching a programme on the television.

Sheila decided to let the subject drop while making tea and putting a few biscuits on a plate for Neil. As she handed him the cup of tea, her father looked straight into Sheila's eyes while taking her hand; she noticed he had tears in his eyes. Neil still sitting, looked up at her earnestly; he smiled at her saying that he was so very sorry for his behaviour and the worry he had caused recently. Still holding her hand tightly, he said that he wouldn't hurt either Rose or her for the world. He also continued saying that he would get some sort of a plan together and that things would change for the better. Sheila, with tears in her eyes, bent down and hugged her father tightly saying it had been an awful ordeal for all of the family. She said that there was nothing for him to be sorry about as she kissed him on the forehead, relieved that he seemed to be in a more positive frame of mind. "Maybe Rose was good for something after all", she thought to herself afterwards.

08

Within a week Neil had disappeared; no one had seen or heard from him, nothing was missing from his room; even his wallet with money in it was on his bedside locker. Sheila was beside herself with worry; the police came around to investigate and a door to door inquiry followed with Garda notices for neighbours to check their outhouses and garden sheds. Nearly every house and business in the Stoneybatter area had a missing poster with a recent photograph of Neil posted in their windows, but no trace of his whereabouts was found.

After months of searching, as the news of Neil's disappearance began to fade, less and less of his missing posters were seen in the local windows; even the police were less active in their search. Sheila, adamant that her father would be found kept up the campaign; she joined a local food shelter serving soup and sandwiches nightly to the homeless in the hope she might spot her father. The army veterans associations, O.N.E. Organisation of National Ex Service Personal, and I.U.N.V.A. Irish United Nations Veterans Association, were a great help as they sent out missing posters of Neil throughout the whole country through their network. Photos of Neil were posted in the north, south, east, and west of Ireland, but still nothing was heard.

About a year later, while Joe was resting off his night shift, a frantic banging started at his front door. As Joe opened his door, Sheila rushed in wide eyed and smiling with an open letter in her hand, saying she had got news of her dad. After wiping the sleep from his eyes, Joe, delighted for Sheila sat down to read the letter. Sheila smiling and clasping her hands together, paced up and down while Joe studied the letter in detail. When he had finished reading, he looked up at Sheila's hopeful face looking back at him; he knew he wasn't as enthusiastic as her about its content but tried to put on a brave face for her anyway.

The letter had come from a private investigation company called Dalton and Dalton situated outside Kilkenny City, Ireland in a small village called Muckalee. It was from a retired army veteran who had seen Neil's missing poster and remembered him as the chef sergeant when he had served with him in Cyprus as a military policeman in the international mess where they ate. He went on to say that when he retired from the army, he and his brother, also a retired military policeman opened their own investigation company. In their investigation of her father's case, they had unearthed some information that may be of some interest to Sheila and would she make contact with them at her convenience. Joe being very cautious didn't want to pour cold water on its contents, so he agreed that it might be the break she was looking for, but he encouraged her to contact Rose to see what she thought. When Sheila showed Rose the letter, she didn't seem at all interested in the news; she said it might be a con-job to extort money out of her, and that Dalton and Dalton might not be even a real company, also to be very careful if they ask for an investigation fee.

As it turned out, Dalton and Dalton was a legitimate investigation company. Although a startup, and from a small village, they were willing to impart the information to Sheila free of charge because Neil was a fellow veteran. They hoped he would be found, but she would have to investigate the information herself, which was in Cyprus. It wasn't easy but Sheila convinced Rose to accompany her to Muckalee to meet with Mr John Dalton to find out what the information was, and why they had to investigate the information themselves. The directions they were given were easy enough to follow; head through Castlecomer Co Kilkenny, and follow the sign for St Brendan's Church in Muckalee, Dalton and Dalton offices were in the community project past the church on the right. From Dublin, it only took about two hours; Sheila was upbeat during the whole journey while Rose just listened to her excited babble as they drove.

When they arrived, they were shown into Mr Dalton's office immediately with the offer of coffee and croissants.

Sheila was impressed with Mr Dalton and could tell he was an ex-soldier by his deportment and neat dress. He had a very friendly demeanour and insisted they both called him John; he politely asked if they had a nice journey down and spoke about the weather. But Sheila cringed when Rose cut across his conversation saying...

"Yeah yeah, but we are here to talk about our father, so could we get down to the business at hand of finding him".

John, taken aback at the interruption, cleared his throat saying, "Yes yes. I'm sure you are very worried about him", as he took a large file from his desk drawer and put his glasses on. When Sheila saw how thick the file was, she thought to herself, there must have been a lot of hours put into the investigation to amass so much information.

09

As the three gathered around the table John, while looking at Rose, explained that in order to give them the information they needed, they would have to bear with him while he went back a few years to the beginning of how they came across the information about their father. He went on to say the information came in two parts.

Part one goes back to the year 1969 in Libya, North Africa. At that time, there was a bloodless coup d'etat called the al Fateh revolution deposing the monarchy in which a Colonel Muammar Gaddafi became the de facto leader. Then in 1973, the R.C.C. Revolutionary Command Council appointed him Brotherly Leader of Libya but he also remained head of both the military and policing committees. Around 1996, an off shore drilling company called Bella Mining Corporation applied for drilling rights off the coast of Libya. To raise funds for this venture, they sold shares on the stock exchange promising large returns when they struck oil. Share prices increased in the company as people began to invest. Bella Mining Corporation started to become a big name in the stock exchange as they began their operations in Libya.

But to get drilling rights, like any multinational corporation, they had to apply through the Libyan government for permission.

At that time Colonel Gaddafi their leader, wanted to build up his military force in North Africa with more men, modern weaponry, and military machinery. To achieve this, he needed funding, so of course the first people he approached were the multi nationals to make a "donation" to his country. Bella Mining Corporation refused to fund his military machine, citing that they would not be involved in war mongering; therefore Colonel Gaddafi refused them their drilling rights.

Within days, the share price in Bella Mining Corporation collapsed on the stock exchange, people and companies lost millions with some going to the wall. Afterwards, when the whole project was abandoned, it was the big investors and creditors who would get a share in what was left. It also looked like the small investors would lose everything. Now, twenty years later, as the company was being wound up, any monies outstanding from this venture was now being paid out to the small investors, which should be little enough.

Rose and Sheila listened intently as John spoke and when he had finished, Sheila asked the question.

"But what would this have to do with our father?" John answered, "This is where part two comes in".

What Dalton and Dalton had uncovered was that a Mr Neil Callery had invested the sum of five thousand

Irish pounds around that time in Bella Mining Corporation from a bank in Cyprus. In our investigations, it turned out that your father was serving there as a cook corporal around that time. There is now a payment due to him from the wind-up company of eleven hundred pounds sterling, five hundred pounds sterling would be paid immediately and a further six hundred pounds sterling approximately would be paid as a final payment when the company closed off their sterling accounts. At this stage, Sheila very confused looked at Rose, who seemed to be as confused as she was, so they both asked the question at the same time.

"But what has that got to do with our missing father?" Sheila continued, "We are only talking about money here, but we need to find out where he is. We don't really care about the money due to him at all".

"Ahh", John said while holding up his hand to stop them talking with a smile on his face. He went on to say that in the last three months, a Mr Neil Callery withdrew five hundred pounds sterling from a bank account in Kyrenia, Northern Cyprus where the local currency is Turkish Lira which would be very unusual. John went on to say that this seemed to be too much of a coincidence given that Callery would be an unusual name there. He told them that Dalton & Dalton had taken the liberty of contacting the Irish military police company presently serving in Nicosia Cyprus to see if they would investigate. Unfortunately, they could not follow it up because of GDPR which is a European General Data Protection Regulation, so our investigation came to a standstill without an account holder's written approval. He also said because we had sent them a copy of the missing poster of Neil Callery, the Military Police would make more copies and initiate a search in Cyprus.

John then finished off by saying, "The reason you both are here today is to acquaint you with the information, and as family members, you might be able to follow up on what happened, and ascertain if it was indeed your father who withdrew the money in Cyprus or somebody purporting to be him".

10

S heila was ecstatic; again all the way home in the car she babbled on at Rose of how they had, "at last" got a lead on their father's whereabouts and proved the theory that he wasn't dead. Rose just rolled her eyes at Sheila saying that the information they had been given proved nothing. Five thousand Irish pounds was a lot of money in those days and knowing their father, he wouldn't take such a gamble and invest a large sum like that on a drilling venture off the north coast of Africa. But Sheila wouldn't be dissuaded no matter what Rose said; she was going to find out if indeed it was her father who withdrew that money.

Immediately on getting home, Sheila contacted the Detective Garda who was handling the case into Neil's disappearance. What she needed was written permission from a judge to go through his accounts in Ireland and abroad. After receiving this permission, she set about forensically going through all his accounts.

After months of trawling through every account, she found that the whole exercise led to nothing. Since Neil's disappearance, not one penny was withdrawn from any bank or credit union account he had. Even his army pension payments that were deposited regularly into his bank account were untouched, and that was amounting to a tidy sum. Worse than that, there was absolutely no information of any account being held by a Mr Neil Callery in Cyprus.

After every avenue was exhausted with no result, it looked like they were back where they started. Rose was only too happy to say, "I told you so" but Sheila wouldn't be deterred. She had already decided as a family member, her only option was to travel to Kyrenia in northern Cyprus and find out any information about Neil's account from the bank where the money was withdrawn. Rose tried to argue the point that they would be wasting their time but Sheila, putting up her hand telling her to stop, saying "no". She continued adamantly that she would bring with her the Garda's missing person's file accumulated over the past two years, plus the judge's written permission to look into the account if there was one, of Mr Neil Callery to help ascertain his whereabouts.

Sheila was taken aback when Rose shouted, "Alright, for fuck's sake, if you insist that you have to go, I'll travel with you, only if it is to put this fucking farce to bed once and for all. Anyway", she continued, "I could do with a bit of a sun holiday to top up my tan".

Two weeks later, Sheila and Rose touched down in Larnaca airport in southern Cyprus. Before they had travelled from Ireland, they contacted IUNVA to see if they could give them practical assistance. As a result, on their arrival, they were greeted by Quartermaster Thomas Mc Cann and his wife Vivienne. They were a lovely friendly couple; Tommy was on duty with the Irish Component serving in a humanitarian role. He told them they had accommodation arranged for them close to the Blue Beret Camp in Nicosia. On the journey from the airport, Vivienne explained how she and their three children were allowed to accompany Tommy while serving with UN-FICYP. His appointment was for over a year and it was accepted that soldier's families could stay with them in British Army Married Quarters in the camp. While serving, it was also arranged that their children would be educated in the local multinational school. She spoke about the many multinational contingents serving in Cyprus, mostly British, Canadian, Swedish, Norwegian, and a small contingent of Irish.

She also very kindly prepared an information package for them telling about the history of the Irish battalions serving in Cyprus for light reading when they reached their hotel. She said they might be able to recognise some of the units their father served with over the years. When they got to the hotel, Tommy said he would return the next day and give them a tour around Nicosia and the Blue Beret Camp. Their father had served on five different trips for six months at a time as cook sergeant.

The boutique hotel was old fashioned but contemporary inside with a bar and small swimming pool, the bedroom was light and airy that was nicely decorated and had air conditioning. As Rose headed down to the bar for a cocktail, Sheila said she wanted a cool shower first and might follow her later. After her shower, Sheila sat back on her bed to browse through the information package Vivienne had given her. Inside the large envelope was a map of Cyprus and various tourist pamphlets of markets, shopping, and sightseeing things to do. Also included was a pamphlet on the history of Irish Battalion's and Infantry Groups serving in Cyprus which she started reading.

The United Nations Peacekeeping Force in Cyprus (UNFICYP) was established in 1964 to prevent violence between Greek Cypriots and Turkish Cypriots. The Irish were represented in peacekeeping by the 40th Infantry battalion who were deployed in April 1964. Following a Greek Cypriot coup d'état in 1974, Turkey invaded the Island of Cyprus when they took the city of Farmagusta under its control dividing the country in two. UNFIC-YP expanded its mission there to patrol a Buffer Zone known as the Green Line which cuts through the centre of Nicosia and northern Cyprus to prevent an all out war between the Greek Cypriots in the south and the Turks in the north. In some parts of the Buffer Zone, Greeks and Turks live side by side in relative peace and the Zone has become a haven for wildlife; to this day the area is still patrolled by UN soldiers. In 1973, the Irish Battalion were re-deployed to the Sinai Desert for peace keeping duty on the Golan Heights because of the Yom Kippur war between Israel and Syria. To this day, Irish Soldiers still serve in Cyprus in humanitarian, logistics, and a military police capacity as part of a multinational peace keeping force.

As Sheila read, memories came flooding back to the sadness she experienced when her father left for UN duty and the great joy of his homecoming after six months of overseas service. Her father would bring presents for everyone and she also remembered her mum and dad behaving like love sick teenagers as they rekindled their love for each other. She especially remembered that on one of his trips when he was away for Christmas, she was about nine years old and was not quite sure if she believed in Santa anymore. As a special treat, her mother had brought her and Rose into town window shopping; it was a wonderful day with the feeling of expectation in the air. They visited the moving crib in Parnell Square, then they went over to Grafton Street to see the lights. It was lovely to listen to the sounds of the various rival carol singers on different parts of the street vying for donations for their own charities.

Afterwards they went into Henry street to see the stall holders lined along the street calling out, "get the last of your cheeky Charlies". It was a toy monkey and mother said they could pick an extra present each. To end the perfect day out, mother brought them both into Cafolla's ice cream parlour for knickerbocker glories. Sheila felt sad that her father had missed such a lovely day out with them so in her letter, she asked Santa to bring her father home for Christmas and knew if it didn't happen, there was no such thing as Santa Claus.

On Christmas morning, she woke to her mother standing over her bed saying, "Look who Santa has brought us?" On running into her parent's bedroom, she was amazed and delighted to see her father lying in bed smiling at her; as she ran to hug and kiss him, she became a believer forever. It was a few years after that she found out that a friend of her father serving with the British Army, who was also a chef had pulled a few strings and had gotten him on a RAF flight from Akrotiri with some British servicemen returning for the Christmas period, but he had to return with them within seven days. As she remembered both her parents with love and affection, Sheila drifted off to sleep.

11

It was in the early hours of the morning when Sheila was awoken by someone at the front bedroom door, she looked over at Rose's bed to see it hadn't been slept in; she could hear laughing in the hallway outside and knew it was her, so she opened the door. As she did so, Rose and a man whom she found out later was the barman, nearly fell into the room; both of them were very intoxicated and started to laugh hysterically. After they both calmed down, Sheila pushed the barman into the hallway and closed the door. She then helped Rose onto the bed removing her shoes but leaving her clothes on and covered her up with a sheet. When she checked the time, it was 2.30 am. The next morning Sheila woke, showered, and prepared for their tour around Nicosia; as she was heading down to breakfast, she shook Rose to get up and get herself ready. Rose just moaned telling Sheila to leave her alone as she turned over for more sleep. It was obvious Rose was hung over so Sheila decided to go down on her own as Tommy wasn't due for another hour or so.

When Tommy arrived, Sheila explained to him that Rose had a bad night, and might not be travelling with them today, but if he would wait a few minutes, she would check to see if she was coming. Tommy gestured there was no problem and to take as long as she needed because it was their day out. When Sheila went up to check on Rose, she was in the bathroom and sounded like she was vomiting. Sheila gently knocked on the door asking if she was ok, and saying that Tommy was downstairs. Rose called out from behind the door to give her fifteen minutes and she would follow her down. As Sheila and Tommy waited in the reception area discussing their plans for the day, Tommy rose from his seat smiling and said Rose had arrived and maybe they should get going.

Sheila couldn't believe her eyes when she turned to see Rose walking up to them looking like a million dollars wearing white shorts, a beautiful pink T shirt knotted above her navel. Around her neck she wore a short scarf knotted to the side, and an elegant straw hat; her eyes were glistening and she wore bright red lipstick, which accentuated her broad smile. Tommy was the perfect guide. He drove them around pointing out historic buildings and places of interest; he gave them an insight into the history of northern and southern Cyprus.

Afterwards, he brought them to the blue beret camp for lunch in the international mess. As they walked around the camp, Sheila realized that Rose was getting a lot of attention from the servicemen. When Rose saw the men looking at her admiringly, she added a little bit of extra wriggle to her walk. Tommy noticed it too and was enjoying himself also as he was getting looks of envy as well.

After lunch, when the servicemen had returned to their duties, Tommy went into the kitchen to tell the chefs that Neil Callery's daughters were visiting. Anyone who remembered Neil came out to reminisce with the girls. Sheila was delighted to hear the kind words each chef conveyed to them and the fond memories they recalled of Neil when they served with him. It was while they spoke of Neil in such a complementary way that Sheila felt very close to her father. It was at this point while thinking of her father that she could feel the hair standing on the back of her neck, which made her shiver.

One chef in particular stood out from the rest; Sheila took an instant dislike to him. She could not quite put her finger on why she disliked him but his mannerisms and the way he spoke to them was different from the others. When Tommy explained to the chefs that Neil was missing, they were all very sympathetic except this one man. When they had all gone back to work, Sheila questioned Tommy asking him who he was. Tommy explained that he was with the British army and was the longest serving chef in the camp with many trips served in Cyprus. He told them his name was Bill Vickers but he was affectionately known as Queenie because he would perform a very funny drag act when the camp put on variety shows for the troops.

Later, Tommy brought them to the military police detachment HQ as he wanted to get the permission slips to cross over into northern Cyprus, which was basically a blue UN pass card. While there, Sheila was taken aback but heartened to see her father's missing persons poster on the wall. The MP Commander explained that although they had no information on his whereabouts, they would still keep the case open.

Tommy was on duty the next couple of days so the girls had time to themselves to go shopping and do a little sunbathing. Sheila enjoyed the old streets of Nicosia and could walk for miles but Rose wanted to visit the gold shops where she bought a very expensive diamond ring saying Frank would have wanted her to have it as she held out the back of her hand to display her new purchase. Sheila thought to herself if Frank could see her flirting with the young barman back at the hotel, would he really have wanted to buy her a ring?

The next day Rose wanted to have what she called "a pool day"; it wasn't Sheila's kind of thing but she felt she should keep her company anyway. Rose lay out in a skimpy thong while covering herself in oil from time to time, enjoying the attention of the admiring glances from the men as they passed by while Sheila sat under an umbrella reading. It was in the afternoon when Sheila awoke to find Rose had disappeared. As she sat reading, she saw Rose come out of an apartment which was not theirs on the other side of the pool with the young barman, smiling and holding hands. Sheila put her book down again and pretended to be asleep as Rose approached; the barman returned to his duties behind the counter waving and blowing kisses at her and Rose returned his gesture.

As Rose resumed her place on the lie low beside her, smiling and sighing, Sheila turned to her saying, "Have you no respect for yourself or Frank?"

Rose looked at Sheila telling her to mind her own fucking business, and maybe a good ride might lighten her up, but the chances were slim given by the dowdy way she dressed anyway. Sheila got up, gathered her things and stormed back to her room; that night not one word passed between them as they got ready for bed.

As usual, Rose started ranting and raving about something or other in the bathroom. When she came out, she was fucking and blinding about a mosquito bite she had gotten right in the centre of her forehead. When Sheila looked to see what she was giving out about, she could see the big red puffy bite that Rose was trying to cover up with makeup. Then Sheila remembered a little rhyme they learned back in their school days and she started to sound it out in her head as she lay down smiling to herself and went to sleep.

Rose was so perfect in every single way.
She had a least a million points and always got straight As.
Then one day it happened, the unthinkable to whit.
Rose the perfect got a great big zit.
Big and round and puffy, it covered half her brow.
Funny thing about it though.
I like her better now.

12

Early the next morning as arranged Sheila and Rose met Tommy and Vivienne in the hotel lobby for their day out crossing the green line and heading to Kyrenia in Northern Cyprus. Sheila was very excited and looked forward to seeing what the Turkish side of the border looked like; she also had all the documentation she needed to find out about her father's bank account. Vivienne being a lovely host brought a picnic basket with cold drinks and fruit so they could stop at the beach for a break during the day. She explained that Kyrenia was a very popular tourist resort, and they could stop off later on in the day for a rest and a swim when their business was complete. Rose was happy with that idea as she had brought her swimming costume, but all Sheila wanted to do was to get to the bank as fast as possible to meet with the bank manager.

After waiting in the bank lobby for what seemed like hours, the two girls were approached by a very stern looking man who escorted them into his office. He listened intently as Sheila presented her case; when she had finished, the bank manager stood up rudely informing the girls that he wouldn't help them as he directed them to leave his office. Sheila protested, but he still refused to give them any information regarding the withdrawal, or even if a person by the name of Mr Neil Callery had ever held an account in the bank. When Sheila tried to show him the missing persons file and the judge's letter, with a wave of his hand he dismissed them saying that it was a European directive and would have no jurisdiction in Turkish law. Sheila was devastated after travelling all this way to be turned away.

As the bank manager stood to escort them out of his office, Sheila stood her ground and refused to leave unless the manager was willing to give them at least some or any information about their father. The manager was getting more and more impatient with her at the scene she was creating. As he put his hand on her arm to get her to stand up, Sheila brushed it away angrily refusing to stand and holding on to the two arms of her chair for support to stay sitting down. Rose tried to reason with her but Sheila still refused to listen. She insisted to the two of them that she was not leaving until she got the information she had come for.

At this time, the manager was at boiling point; his face was purple with rage as he went behind his desk once more and sat down. He picked up his phone and spoke in Turkish to someone on the other end of the line as the two girls watched him, Sheila still adamant she was not moving. After about fifteen minutes had passed with the manager staring at them without saying a word, Sheila presumed he was waiting for the information to be delivered to his office as she sat there in front of him.

Then without warning, two armed Turkish policemen burst into the office. Rose, still standing, was roughly pushed up against the wall while being handcuffed; before Sheila could protest, she was grabbed from the chair and thrown face down on the floor. She thought her arm would break as the policeman pulled it up from behind to handcuff her too; he then shoved his knee into the base of her spine to pin her down and keep her from moving. At this stage, a third policeman had entered the room; he held Rose against the wall while the other two dragged Sheila from the floor by her two arms cuffed behind her back as she cried out in pain from the way they had manhandled her. When they had her standing, the policeman grabbed her hair from behind pulling her head back while twisting her arms up behind her back so she would be subdued and motionless as the bank manager came around from behind his desk to face her.

As Sheila looked at him wide eyed and speechless, the bank manager glared at her with a smirk on his face, as he said to her with menace in his voice, "So you presume to think you can come into my bank and demand information you are not entitled to, and then by having a silly childish tantrum, you would hold me to ransom? You stupid girl, who do you think you are?" As he finished speaking to her, he directed the policemen to take her out of his sight.

Sheila and Rose were physically dragged from his office out through the bank lobby and out into the bright sunlight that blinded them both; they were thrown into a waiting police van with its blue light flashing on the roof. Crowds had gathered to view the spectacle thinking it was a bank heist, and while the crowd stood looking on, so too did Tommy and Vivienne totally dumbstruck to see the two girls being taken away in handcuffs. When the girls reached the police station, they were taken into separate holding cells in the back. Sheila felt the shiver of dread as the heavy steel cell door was banged shut behind her.

As her eyes adjusted to the light in the cell, she looked around to see a single bed with dirty blankets and pillow; there was a dirty toilet in the corner and a wash hand basin covered in rust. As she sat on the edge of the bed, the realisation of what had happened hit her as she started to cry into her lap. She then thought about Rose and was worried sick about what might happen to her and the danger she had put her in. She imagined all sorts of terrible things happening to her sister because of the way she was dressed.

After about what felt like hours, a policeman opened the door and without saying a word, he left a bottle of water and some biscuits beside her on the bed; he then left again banging the door behind him. Sheila feeling very thirsty, reached over for the water and as she did so, she winced at the pain in her shoulder and back from when the policemen manhandled her from the bank. As she sat in the fading light of the evening, she thought to herself what was to become of her and her sister and how did she ever end up in a place like this so far from home?

13

Tommy and Vivienne didn't know what to do after watching the girls being led out of the bank in handcuffs. They discussed between themselves about what action to take. Should they head back to UN Headquarters and report what had happened, or should they go to the police station and find out why the girls were arrested. They had decided on the latter and planned that Tommy would go into the police station while Vivienne waited outside in the car and if he didn't come out after an hour, Vivienne was to return to UN Headquarters and report what had happened to the camp company commander.

When Tommy entered the police station, he identified himself while producing his UN identification card. He explained to the police sergeant why he was there and his association with the girls who were being held. He inquired as to why they were arrested and what was the charge; he also wanted to be able to speak to them and check on their welfare. Realizing the girls were involved with the United Nations in Nicosia, the sergeant asked him to wait while he consulted with his officer as to what information he could give him. Within a few minutes he returned, and informed Tommy that the girls would be held overnight as they waited to find out if the bank manager wished to bring charges for the disruption of business in his bank. He gave Tommy permission to visit the girls for five minutes each in their respective cells. Tommy followed the sergeant to Rose's cell first; when inside, he informed her that they would have to stay until tomorrow when they would be told if formal charges would be brought against them. Rose seemed to be ok with that and apologised to Tommy for the ridiculous situation he found himself and Vivienne in as she explained what had happened in the manager's office and how stupid Sheila had behaved. Tommy accepted her apology saying he would come back first thing in the morning after reporting back to UN Headquarters.

As his five minutes was up, he went to see Sheila and found her hysterical in her cell as he walked in. He calmed her down as best he could informing her that Rose was fine and in good spirits. He gave her the same information he gave Rose and again promised her he would be back first thing in the morning as he checked his watch to make sure he hadn't gone over the hour in the police station knowing Vivienne would be waiting for him outside.

There was little sleep for Sheila that night in her dingy little cell. When she had drifted off to sleep on one occasion, she felt something walking on her arm; she opened her eyes to see a big cockroach staring back at her. In a panic, she jumped up to get the horrible thing off her; as it fell to the floor, she could see it running away into a corner where there were others hiding as well. The thought of them on her body made her shiver all over as she drew her knees into her chest to keep her feet off the floor.

When Tommy and Vivienne got back to headquarters, he reported immediately to Colonel William Drake the Camp Commander, filling him in on every detail of what had happened. Colonel Drake contacted the UN Legal Officer and had a Canadian military police Captain by the name of Mark Trimblay who was also a solicitor immediately assigned to the case.

It was arranged that the following morning, both captain Trimblay and quartermaster Mc Cann would return to the police station and ascertain what charges would be brought against the two girls and find out if bail could be arranged for their release if there was to be a trial. In the meantime, Colonel Drake would contact his counterpart on the Turkish side to ascertain if the situation could be resolved amicably.

As it happened, he was informed that the bank manager would not be bringing any charges against the girls as he wanted to teach the girls a lesson in respect when dealing with any Turkish governmental official. The case would be regarded as a misdemeanour but they wanted the girls' blue cards confiscated, then taken from Turkish jurisdiction with strict conditions that they would not be allowed to cross back over the Northern border again.

Very early the next morning, Captain Trimblay and Tommy arrived at the police station to meet the girls waiting in an interview room with the Turkish police captain. Captain Trimblay signed the official document releasing the girls into his custody for transportation back to the southern side of the border by a police and military escort.

Sheila felt it surreal as they travelled from Kyrenia to Nicosia in convoy led by a police car; in the middle was Captain Trimblay and Tommy with the two girls seated in the back, followed by the last vehicle, a military jeep with four armed soldiers. When they reached the border, the girls were processed across where they had their blue cards confiscated.

14

After crossing the border in Nicosia, they were immediately brought back to the blue beret camp to be examined by Major Alexander Phillips a British army medical officer. He was happy with the girls' condition; a few bruises here and there were nothing to worry about, but he thought that Sheila seemed a bit agitated after her ordeal and prescribed her some sedatives. Rose on the other hand loved the attention they were getting; she felt they were like celebrities. She even invited the handsome young Captain Trimblay back to her hotel that night for drinks as she had noticed he wasn't wearing a wedding ring, but he declined graciously citing that he had to attend to his duties.

Later, they were taken back to the dining hall for a lavish lunch. Bill Vickers, the chef sergeant was there in his immaculate chef's whites; he was of average build, balding, with bow shaped lips, bulging eyes with elongated eye lashes and he was fussing all over them. He was treating them like royalty while trying to glean any information he could about their ordeal so he could spread the gossip around the camp which annoyed Sheila all the more. Tommy, noticing Sheila's annoyance whispered in her ear not to be too hard on him because when Bill found out that they were in trouble, he came to Tommy's house in married quarters the night before. He had offered to pay for any legal fees or fines that may have been required by the Turkish authorities, or indeed any help the girls might have needed, which surprised her immensely.

Sheila was glad to be back in the dining hall after her ordeal because it was here that she felt her father's presence, which did help in reducing the disappointment of not getting any information about him. She felt that the whole journey was just a waste of time, expense, and knew that this was the end of the line. She also knew that Rose would be just waiting to say, "I told you so" but at this moment, Rose said nothing as she was just enjoying all the attention being lavished on her.

On returning to the hotel, Sheila went straight to her room while Rose thanked Tommy and Vivian for a most interesting day. When she knew that Sheila was out of earshot, she told them that to her, her father was dead. She said that Sheila was on a knife edge worrying about him, so if any more information emerged about stocks shares or anything that was uncorroborated, she would prefer if they didn't pass it on.

That night, the two girls lay sleepless while thinking about their separate adventures. Rose thought about what she had confided in Tommy and hoped that would be the last of this stupid running around looking for information. Sheila thought about how while standing in the camps kitchens where her father had worked, she had felt so very near to him there. She also thought about Bill Vickers and how she took an instant dislike to him. It wasn't because he was gay, but he stood back from the other chefs and didn't want to engage with them at all until they were arrested and brought back to the camp for lunch. She also wondered why he would want to help them with the Turkish authorities, but let the thought pass.

It was at the end of their holiday when Sheila had her breakdown. After being dropped off at Larnica airport by Tommy, Sheila, still very agitated over their ordeal was still apologising over and over again for the trouble she had caused to Tommy and Vivienne who were so nice to them on their trip. Tommy just accepted her apology saying not to worry about it and to have a safe trip home. While waiting to board their flight home, the mood lightened a little and the girls started talking. During the conversation, when there was a short lull, Sheila turned to Rose asking, "Did you feel dad's presence like I did in the military kitchen in Nicosia?" While smiling, she continued "I somehow felt very near to him there".

With that, Rose exploded saying, "For fuck's sake Sheila, will you just get a grip and shut the fuck up about dad being near? You know like I do that he is dead".

"You have dragged me half way across Europe on some wild goose chase because YOU got some poxy information from some poxy fly by night private Detective Company giving you false hope that we might find him. Then you had me thrown into a poxy Turkish prison because you wanted to have a tantrum to try and bully the bank manager. So now, shut the fuck up, as I don't want to hear another fucking word from you on the flight home about a feeling YOU had about dad being near".

When Rose had finished her rant, the only words that kept ringing through Sheila's ears was, "YOU KNOW LIKE I DO THAT DAD IS DEAD"...

The words kept going around and around her head again and again; she could feel the room spinning as she started to cry out louder and louder...

"He is not dead, he is not dead, HE IS NOT DEAD", until it became a scream...

"HE IS NOT DEAD"...

Sheila couldn't stop herself; people were looking over at them concerned. Rose was shouting at her to stop, until she slapped her across the face as hard as she could to get her to snap out of it; when the slap hit Sheila, it felt like a rocket had exploded in her head and she passed out. When Sheila came around, Rose was sitting beside her; she told her the flight had left without them as they had a schedule to keep.

The rep also told her if she wanted to book a flight at a later date, they would have to get Sheila assessed by a doctor and obtain a letter that she was mentally fit to travel. So Rose contacted Tommy humbly telling him what had happened and why they had missed their flight. Tommy and Vivienne were wonderful; Tommy came back to the airport and picked them up, while Vivienne rebooked the same room in the hotel, and over the next couple of days, they organised the camp medical officer to assess Sheila and provide her with a fitness to fly certificate. Sheila, apologetic and totally deflated, accepted anything Rose suggested just to get finished with her and the whole sorry escapade in Cyprus.

When she got home, Joe was waiting and anxious to hear all her news, but when he saw her sad and sorrowful face, he knew the news was bad and decided not to speak about her adventure in Cyprus. Although he had made a welcome home banner and had prepared a nice supper, Sheila said she was exhausted and just wanted to go to bed. That night in the quietness of her room, Sheila cried into her pillow at what seemed was the end of her search for her father. Joe, hearing her through the wall next door, let his tears quietly fall onto his pillow as he also wept for his friend who was so distraught.

15

As the years passed, Neil Callery's name was used less and less as the acceptance of his disappearance became final. Sheila carried on working in Tommy O' Gara's pub as normal, living alone in Oxmanstown Road next door to Joe. Rose and Sheila's relationship became non-existent.

Early one morning, Sheila woke up with a sore throat and a blinding headache and as she felt she was developing a cold and could pass it on to her work colleagues, she rang Tommy O' Gara to explain how she was feeling. Tommy was a decent skin and knew Sheila was a good and honest worker, so he told her to take the day off and make herself plenty of hot drinks; he also asked Sheila if she would like her dinner dropped up to her house from the lunch time menu. Sheila accepted gladly knowing she had nothing in the fridge for dinner as she had expected to be working and would have gotten her dinner there, as the staff usually ate in the pub when the busy lunch time was over.

When the call ended, Sheila made herself a hot drink, took some paracetamol and went back to bed hoping to sleep it off. It must have been around midday when Sheila was awoken from a deep sleep by somebody inserting a key in her front door and coming into her hallway. She knew that Joe was working his day shift that week and he was the only person with a spare key in case of emergencies or if she had locked herself out of the house, and she kept his key for the same reason. Sheila also knew that Joe would never use her key without getting permission from her first to drop into the hallway any large parcels or deliveries that would not fit through her letter box, and she also knew she hadn't ordered anything on line recently.

As Sheila lay in the bed with the covers pulled up to her chin, fear and panic started to take over her. She felt sick to her stomach as she realized she had left her mobile phone charging down in the kitchen and had no other way in calling for help. She could hear footsteps walking around downstairs, so she decided to creep over to her bedroom door and have a look to see who or where they were in the house. She knew that if they went into the back kitchen, she might be able to run downstairs and straight out the front door to a neighbour's house for help. Her heart was pounding as she positioned herself to execute her escape plan when she heard a male voice she did not recognise; just then a female voice answered him and she knew exactly who it was.

Without saying a word, Sheila crept down the stairs through the hallway and stood with her hands on her hips looking down at Rose and a strange man sitting at her kitchen table. Neither of them saw her as the man had his head down and was writing into some sort of journal. Rose had her back to Sheila and she was watching what he wrote down. When the man was finished, he lifted his head to speak to Rose saying.

"I think this would be a really quick and profitable sale". Just then he saw Sheila standing in the doorway and stopped talking as he smiled at her. Rose knowing there was someone behind her swung around to see Sheila standing there; the look of surprise on her face said it all. She didn't expect Sheila to be in the house; as the two girls' eyes met, Rose tried to break the awkward silence by introducing the man.

"Eh, eh, Sheila this is Mister Michael Reilly of Reilly Estate Agents".

"Mr Reilly, this is my sister Sheila".

Mr Reilly rose from his seat saying how happy he was to meet her; he also continued saying how pleased he was to view their lovely home with which he would expect to make a very quick sale with a very nice return for both of them as Cowtown was becoming a very popular and fashionable area to buy. Sheila didn't say a word; she just kept staring at her sister waiting for an explanation as to what was going on?

Rose still embarrassed at being caught decided to take charge of the situation. She turned to Mr Reilly, saying loudly. "Thank you Mr Reilly for your visit and we will be in touch as soon as we have decided whether we would require your service or not".

Mr Reilly, still standing could feel the tension in the air; he was going to ask if they wanted to show him the two bedrooms upstairs so he could take measurements. But looking at the girls' faces, he decided to leave the question unsaid; he then closed his journal stating that he would leave his business card on the table as he made a hasty retreat out the front door closing it firmly behind him.

16

Cowtown as Mr Reilly called it was indeed becoming a very popular area and in particular Oxmanstown Road was fetching premium prices at the moment. The word Cowtown was used to describe the area of North Circular Road around Hanlon's Corner where weekly cattle markets would be held in the fifties, sixties, and seventies. Drovers would herd their cattle and sheep through the streets of Dublin City from the dockland and surrounding country areas to sell their beasts. All around the local area were abattoirs waiting for the purchase and sale of the animals that would be brought straight to them for slaughter. It provided many jobs in the area where butchers and drovers settled down and bought houses. Some families of up to thirteen people lived in those two up, two down houses with an outside toilet in the back yard.

Now that same area is being bought up by high tech yuppies paying a premium price because of its proximity to the city centre and law library. When a sale goes through, the house is usually gutted and that same house becomes an architect designed bijou residence. The cattle market is long gone now, replaced by a modern estate of three and four bedroom houses. When Mr Reilly had left and closed the front door firmly behind him, the standoff continued between the two girls. Eventually Sheila decided to speak, asking the question.

"What are you up to now, Rose?"

Rose, knowing she was caught red handed decided to brazen it out saying that she just wanted to get a ballpark figure on how much a property like theirs would be worth if ever they decided to sell the house in the future.

Sheila asked, "Why would we ever consider selling the family home, and to imagine what dad would think when he decided to come back home? Just think about it for a moment, he would have nowhere to live".

Rose replied while standing up and gathering her things to leave that it was only an idea in case he didn't come back. Sheila was flabbergasted at such a suggestion and replied to Rose.

"Don't even think like that Rose, we will find him and everything will go back to normal, you wait and see".

With that Rose said impatiently, "Yeah yeah, but we should keep all our options open", as she picked up her car keys to leave.

Just then there was a knock on the door and it was Joan delivering her lunch from the pub. Rose, realizing that Sheila was off work sick understood why she had been caught viewing the house. She turned to Sheila asking if she was alright or needed anything? Sheila knowing it was an empty gesture declined her offer and Rose left.

Afterwards, while Sheila ate her lunch alone, she tried to make sense of the morning's encounter, but as she had a splitting headache and had lost her appetite, she decided to take two more paracetamols and go back to bed. As she headed upstairs with her mobile phone in her hand, she stopped at the front door and slid across the deadbolt, something that she couldn't remember doing in her lifetime. She also made a note in her head to call into Threshold, a citizens' advise bureau next door to Tommy O Gara's; she knew the girls there well as they were regulars in the pub.

It was in about the sixth year of Neil's disappearance Rose made it known that when the seventh year had passed and Neil was declared legally dead, she wanted to get a death certificate. Then as soon as possible after that, the house would be sold and any assets left would be divided equally between the two girls. Sheila devastated at this news, confided in Joe that with the rising price of houses and the shortage of property in the North Dublin area, and being on a single person's wage, she doubted she would be able to buy out Rose's share of the house. She also said it would kill her if the family home was sold out from under her, which would make her virtually homeless. As he held her hand, Joe acted all concerned for Sheila, but Joe was secretly absolutely delighted with this news. He knew there would never be a better time to ask Sheila to marry him, but for now, he would wait for the opportune time to ask her.

As it happened, he didn't have long to wait. Rose had engaged a solicitor to act on her behalf, and as they were sisters, the same solicitor had written to Sheila as well asking if she too would like to engage his services. Sheila had asked the girls in Threshold for advice but they could not give her any as that they only dealt with people who were tenants, and as she would become a co-owner of the house after the seventh year, she would have to get legal advice from a solicitor. Anyway Sheila knew in fairness, she would never stop the sale of the house going through if her sister wanted her share as she felt she would be entitled to it. So Sheila, sick with worry called into Joe to show him the solicitor's letter; this heightened her anxiety that the house would be sold out from under her.

Joe, feeling the time was right, with his heart beating uncontrollably in his chest took Sheila's hand in his, looking earnestly into her eyes saying... "My darling Sheila, I have lived beside and loved you since we were children. If you moved away from me, my heart would just wither and die. If you were to marry me, I would cherish you forever, look after you, and you would never have to worry about where you would live for the rest of your life".

A silence fell on the moment, which seemed like a lifetime for Joe as he waited for her answer with bated breath. Sheila eventually looked into his eyes; Joe's heart was pounding as he waited expectantly. Eventually, Sheila smiled at Joe; taking his face in both her hands, she kissed him on the mouth. Joe thought he would die as Sheila hugged him and whispered gently in his ear...

"Joe, oh Joe, you must be the most wonderful friend anyone could ever have, to say those beautiful words to me when I was feeling so low. I will always love you for this beautiful moment but I couldn't possibly marry you just to get a roof over my head".

Poor Joe's heart sunk for he knew the moment of his proposal was lost; he mustered up a smile and said...

"If ever you change your mind the offer is always there, or even if you need somewhere to live, I have a spare bedroom".

Sheila responded saying, "Don't worry Joe, I will think of something", as she kissed him on the cheek again.

But Joe did worry; he worried that his friend might move away from him forever, and that would break his heart.

17

A month later, Sheila called into Joe to ask him if he would be available to give her and Joan, her co-worker a lift to the airport. They had both had a week's holiday coming and had decided to book a trip together to Tenerife; Joe agreed and said he would also pick her up on her return. On the day of her departure, Joe chatted to Sheila in the car as they drove to the airport, but he felt that Sheila was very quiet and distant on the journey out. As he waved her off at the terminal, Sheila who should have been happy to be starting a sunshine holiday with her friend looked at Joe in a way that sent shivers down his spine. Joe feared there was something wrong but what it was escaped him at that moment.

Joe's fears were realised when Sheila didn't return the following week; he decided to contact Rose about his worries as she might be having another breakdown. It was then Rose told him to mind his own fucking business and keep out of their family affairs. Sheila hated lying to Joe or even keeping him out of the loop, but she didn't want to worry him or worse still, for him to try and talk her out of travelling to Tenerife after what happened in Cyprus four years previously. She also feared he might contact Rose to try and stop her, so her best option was to do this thing alone without any interference from anyone. Her friend Joan travelling with her was a complete accident; she had seen Sheila reading a lonely planet book on Tenerife and invited herself along. Joan remarked that she and her husband Eddie had spent their honeymoon in Tenerife and always wanted to go back. When Sheila said that she was considering a short holiday, Joan jumped in and said that if she was looking for a travelling companion to keep her in mind as Eddie didn't really like flying. So, considering it would make her trip look legitimate as two friends going on a girlie holiday, Sheila feeling a little guilty, suggested Joan should come with her. As things were quiet in Tommy O' Gara's pub around that time, the girls had no problem getting the same week off together. Also getting a last minute deal for one week staying at the Commadore apartments Los Christianos, proved to be the perfect spot where Sheila wanted to base herself for what she needed to do.

The flight of four hours to Reina Sofia airport and transfers to their apartment went without a hitch. The minute they arrived, Sheila fell in love with Tenerife and Los Christianos in particular. She loved the idea that it once was a small fishing village, but now had a bustling harbour with a long promenade of restaurants and shops to explore. There was also a ferry nearby where one could go on an excursion to the neighbouring island of La

Gomera and hoped she had time to venture over later in the week, but for now she had business to attend to first.

That first night, the girls got dressed up and went out for dinner and of course a few drinks. Taking in the sights and sounds of the busy bars and cafes lit up at night offering typical Canarian dishes was an absolute delight. But all the while, Sheila was making mental notes of the surrounding area and where she wanted to be the next day without Joan.

The next morning, Sheila was up early as she was excited about her business she had to conduct during the day. After breakfast, Joan said she wanted to sit by the pool and make a start on her tan. Sheila said that she would like to go for a walk and take a look around the shops, so both girls agreed they would meet up for lunch when Sheila got back.

As soon as Sheila left the apartment, she headed straight for the Banco Vistasur Canarias on the corner of Juan Carlos Avenue opposite the market square in Los Christianos. She knew exactly where she wanted to be from her observations the previous night and had taken note of the bank opening times. In her bag, she carried her father's missing person's file with his photograph, the original letter from the judge, copies of the police investigation into her father's disappearance, and most importantly, a recent letter from Dalton and Dalton private investigators. The letter to Sheila stated that the sum of €730 euro was withdrawn from the Banco Vistasur in the account name of a Mr Neil Callery, eight weeks previously.

When Sheila received the letter from Dalton and Dalton informing her of the withdrawal, she thought it was some sort of cruel joke and was very sceptical about following it up. After careful consideration, she decided to contact Mr Dalton to find out if it was him who sent the letter. Mr Dalton explained that when there was no further information on her father's disappearance, they had decided to archive his missing person's file, but while doing so, they noticed an anomaly. In this anomaly, it came to light that a Mr Neil Callery had withdrawn €730 in euro at the Banco Vistasur only eight weeks previously. When Mr Dalton calculated the exchange rate from sterling to euro, it amounted to what was owed on the account that was due to the Turkish Bank in Cyprus from Bella Mining Corporation. He told her that like before, it seemed too much of a coincidence for him not to convey this information to her if indeed she wished to follow it up. Sheila thanked him profusely saying that she certainly would look into it and asked him if he was owed money for their investigations. Mr Dalton reiterated that there was no charge for their services as her father was a fellow veteran; he also wished her the best of luck in her search as the call ended.

18

Sheila entered the bank and asked to meet with the manager; the bank assistant inquired if she had an appointment, Sheila told her she hadn't. The assistant then asked the nature of her inquiry, as maybe she could handle it herself. Sheila thanked the assistant for her offer but said she would rather speak to the bank manager as it was a delicate matter. Looking a little concerned, the assistant asked her to take a seat while she checked if the manager would be able to see her today.

As she took her seat, Sheila noticed the blind being lifted a little so the bank manager could observe her as the assistant spoke. Then the assistant returned and explained to her that the manager was in a meeting but when she had finished, she would see her if she wished to wait. Sheila checked her watch and as she had plenty of time before lunch with Joan, she agreed to wait awhile longer. About forty minutes later, the manager approached apologising for holding her so long as she was on a zoom call. Sheila thought her approach was lovely and said...

"Considering I have no appointment, I didn't mind waiting".

The bank manager introduced herself as Conchita Martinez and invited Sheila into her office. As Sheila stood up, she thought to herself, what a difference to meeting this lady in comparison to her last encounter with the bank manager in Cyprus and relaxed totally as she entered. Once inside her office, Sheila sat down while Conchita closed some drawers in a filing cabinet that were left ajar. As she turned to approach her desk, Sheila looked up to admire this lovely lady who was tall and slim with shining black hair tied up in a bun; she wore a beautiful formal business suit over a crisp white blouse.

As Conchita sat down, she smiled at Sheila asking her what could she help her with? Sheila opened her file and told her from start to finish the whole sorry story of her missing father, the ill treatment she received at the bank in Cyprus, and even about her breakdown afterwards.

Conchita listened intently without interruption showing empathy and concern as Sheila passed her the judge's letter, photos of her father, and the evidence given to her from Dalton and Dalton. When Sheila had finished speaking, she wiped her eyes as Conchita handed her a tissue saying how sorry she was, and waited until she regained her composure. Conchita then gently asked her if she would like some water or maybe coffee? Sheila declined gratefully but thanked her for her kindness in the way she listened to her story.

Conchita suggested that if Sheila agreed, she would hang on to her file for a couple of days so she could contact

the bank's legal department. She continued that she needed direction in how much information they could impart with regard to any bank customer and the European
General Data Protection Regulation. She also said that
she would show her father's photo to her bank assistants
in case they might recognise him. As Conchita picked up
the file, she looked at Neil's photo and said with a smile...

"He was a handsome man".

Sheila smiled back saying the photo was an old one
but it was the clearest one they had for inclusion into
the file. Conchita sat back in her chair and asked Sheila
if she was enjoying her stay in Tenerife; she also asked
where she was staying in case they wanted to contact her.
Sheila, a little more relaxed, told her how she had fallen in
love with the island the minute they had landed; she also
told her where she was staying and her room number. She
was a little surprised when Conchita asked her if she had
tried any of the local bars and restaurants in the area. She
said there were some great value meals and some of the
bars had free entertainment included. Sheila said that she
would keep that in mind as they had the full week ahead
of them to explore.

As the meeting ended, Conchita stood up and escorted Sheila to the door; shaking hands, they said goodbye
for now. When Sheila exited the bank, she was elated; she
felt this was the first time she had felt that maybe, just
maybe, she wasn't making a complete fool of herself and
in a few days, she might get some positive answers at last.

Over the next few days, Sheila and Joan had a great time together shopping, exploring, and sun bathing; every night they would visit the local area enjoying the shows and generally enjoying each other's company.

Towards the end of the week, while Joan was visiting the market to get the last few presents before going home, Sheila slipped away and returned to the bank. On meeting with Conchita, she was escorted into her office and sat down waiting expectantly with bated breath. Conchita opened her file and began to say that she had contacted the legal department with all her information and they were very moved by her sad story. She told her they did agree that they could give her some of the information she required but...

At this point, Sheila put up her hands to cover her mouth to stop herself from crying out, but Conchita stopped her saying that they had only some information that they could impart.

As Sheila waited for this information, Conchita while staring at her and speaking softly, continued, "I am sorry but unfortunately, the money that was withdrawn from this bank was not that of your father Mr Neil Callery". Sheila, looking devastated and couldn't believe what she was hearing, but Conchita continued before she could be interrupted.

There was a transfer into this bank for the sum of €730 Euro in the name of Mr Neil Callery but the withdrawal was made legally to a Mr Neil Callery-Vickers;

Sheila looked at Conchita totally confused. So Conchita explained sadly to her that she was very sorry but because of GDPR, the banks were not at liberty to give any information as to the persons who withdrew the money. As she had finished speaking to Sheila, she started to close the file in preparation to hand it back to her; Sheila, totally dumbstruck just sat in her seat.

As Conchita handed over the file to her, she said after a short pause, but, there is some information you should know that has nothing to do with GDPR. Sheila looked at her expectantly as Conchita told her she had handed around her father's photograph to her staff and one girl did seem to think she recognised him. Although the photo was old, it was his accent she remembered most of all as she felt he could be Irish.

19

Sheila didn't know how to process this information, she felt she needed time alone to analyse it as best she could. She thanked Conchita for her help and candour and asked, if needed, could she return to her at a later stage although she knew there would not be much point. Conchita said to call in any time as she walked her to the door, but this time she didn't shake hands with Sheila as before; she kissed her on the cheek as they parted and Sheila returned her kiss. When Sheila exited the bank, she didn't know which way to turn or whether to laugh or cry; she stood in the street totally confused as she touched her cheek where Conchita had kissed her.

As the holiday came to an end, the girls were due to fly home late that evening. They had decided to visit the Sunday morning market as Joan wanted to have a last look around and get something for Eddie. Sheila said she would get Joe a new leather belt as a thank you for picking her up from the airport. The girls split up and agreed to meet at the sea front overlooking the harbour; they both liked it as it was a good spot for people watching as they walked along the promenade and one could get a nice breakfast and coffee for around €3.50. Sheila arrived first and got a nice table in the shade. After ordering a cold drink, she took out Joe's belt to admire the nice buckle that she knew he would like, happy in the knowledge she had got a bargain. As she sat there sipping her drink, her thoughts turned to her father; she still had no real information that would lead her to him as she thought to herself, "Maybe he is lost forever".

But she would never believe he was dead; she always felt that she would know in her heart if he was, and that feeling just wasn't there. As she sat enjoying the morning atmosphere, she overheard a man say, "Adios Amigo", to a waiter, and her blood ran cold.

She spun around to see who it was but the glare of the sun in her eyes obscured her vision; she stood up to look at the man but he was already walking away with his back to her. Even though the man had spoken in Spanish, his voice was unmistakable and sounded like her father's; something told her to follow him as her heart began to race. She excused herself as she rushed through the tables to reach him as he turned up towards the market square. Frantically, she tried to catch up but the crowds swallowed him up as he disappeared. Sheila returned to the busy restaurant demanding from the waiter who that person was. The waiter, not knowing who she was talking about and thinking she was a mad woman, just shrugged his shoulders and continued serving tables.

Sheila sat down again thinking to herself, had she been mistaken? Was she just clutching at straws? Or worse still, was she having another breakdown like she had in Cyprus? But the man sounded so much like her father even if he did speak Spanish. When she followed him, she could see he was the same height, and walked in the same way with his long stride. His hair was long and curly and he wore a sleeveless vest with pink shorts, a leather anklet above soft deck shoes with no socks.

She thought again, "How could it be him?" He would be far too conservative to be dressed like that, but her mind was still racing, "Was it him?"

Just then Joan arrived; she looked at Sheila's face and asked, "What's the matter? You look like you've seen a ghost", as she sat down while calling the waiter to order breakfast.

As Joan chatted about what she had bought in the market, Sheila was a million miles away, still asking the question to herself, "Was it him?" and why did it have to happen today when she had no time left to check it out.

Is she really having a breakdown? What if she went home without finding out? Then she would never know, but... "Was it him?"

On the journey to the airport, her mind kept racing, asking the same question over and over, "was it him?", would this be her last chance to find her dad? She knew if she boarded the flight home, there would be no going back; the search would end, her father would be declared dead, the house would be sold, and she would be made homeless. She closed her eyes and prayed for guidance,

God help me what am I going to do?

By the time they reached the airport, her mind was made up; right or wrong, she had to go back and check, even if it was to save her own sanity. Sheila knew she was not having a nervous breakdown; also it was not knowing that would drive her mad altogether.

Sheila was going back...

20

It was Joe's day off and he had prepared a list of jobs in his head he wanted to do around the house, as he started his tasks, he heard a knock on the door. He opened the door and was surprised to see Frank standing there without Rose; Frank asked if he could come in as he needed to discuss something with Joe, so he stood back and let Frank pass.

When they were in the kitchen, Joe put on the kettle thinking Frank was there to admonish him for phoning Rose about Sheila. Joe turned, explaining to Frank that he didn't want to upset anyone but he thought it was his duty to let Rose know that Sheila was in Tenerife and he was very worried that she might be having another breakdown. Joe also said he had contacted Joan, Sheila's workmate and travelling companion who told him what had happened at the airport terminal.

Frank listened for a while before telling Joe that Rose didn't know he was here and would prefer if it was left that way. When Joe looked confused by Frank's statement, he explained that he had been listening when Joe had contacted Rose about Sheila. He said he was disgusted at the tirade of abuse Rose had given him over the phone in telling him to mind his own business when the only thing he cared about was Sheila's welfare. Frank said that Joe was a very good friend to Sheila and felt somehow if they both put their heads together, they might be able to help her. He continued saying that they would have to act quickly as Sheila's condition could deteriorate and God only knows what might happen to her or she might even disappear like Neil.

Joe sat up in his chair, more worried than ever at what Frank had to say. He asked, "But what can we do? She is so far away".

Frank stared Joe in the face and said, "You will have to follow her over there".

Joe couldn't believe his ears; after thinking about Frank's suggestion for a second, he almost laughed as he said, "You must be joking. How can I follow Sheila to Tenerife when I have never been out of the country. I don't possess a passport, what's more I don't even know where Tenerife is. For God's sake Frank, is that the best idea you could come up with?"

Frank, calming him down explained, "Look Joe, it has to be you, Sheila trusts you. If I turned up, she would think Rose sent me and that might make things difficult; also if Rose found out what I was up to, it could make things worse. With regard to your passport, you could apply for an emergency one and it would arrive within ten days, if not sooner. I'll arrange flights and accommodation where Sheila is staying; you keep in contact with me, and if she is ok, you can both fly home together, so what do you think?"

Joe thought for a while, then let out a sigh of acceptance saying, "God Frank, this is mad, but if it means we are helping Sheila, then I'll go".

"Good man", said Frank, as he reached over and slapped him on the shoulder.

Joe said, "I just hope I'm not too late and she is still there when I arrive".

Frank said he would contact the hotel and forward payment for Sheila to stay on until he arrived. So they both agreed with the plan and Rose would never suspect anything. Within a few days, Frank's plan was coming together; Joe had applied for his emergency passport and flights were booked. He contacted the hotel and ascertained that Sheila was still staying there; when this was confirmed, he forwarded payment for her to continue on, as well as booking a room for Joe.

21

As Frank sat back in his office chair, he began to think about Rose and his mind wandered back to when they first met, the sex, the fun, her energy and drive; she was like a dynamo. He tried to remember when or why she had turned so bitter and mean, especially to her only sister Sheila.

He thought about their wedding day; how she arranged every detail and how impressed he was at her organisational skills. How fit she became when she joined the country club winning prizes all around her, and constantly working out to keep her beautiful figure.

When Frank suggested that maybe they should start a family, Rose just laughed it off saying, "And ruin this beautiful body that I have worked so hard to keep". So that was the end of our baby plan as Rose had dictated.

He remembered as he started to climb the ladder of success in his company, his pride in her as she made an entrance into any corporate function looking absolutely fabulous. As he watched her adoringly mingle among the guests, he noticed after a while that people would drift away from her company to gather elsewhere, which bothered him a little. He never really noticed how over the years, they themselves had also drifted apart. They became like ships in the night passing each other in the house. Rose rushing out to some golf tournament or fitness session in the gym,

Frank checking his figures and work load for the next day. It all happened one morning while Frank was in his office overlooking the river liffey; his CEO phoned him from a golf club on the south side of the city. He informed Frank that they were playing a four ball while having an important business meeting with a high ranking executive. Unfortunately, a member of their team had to pull out due to illness and Frank's name was suggested to take his place. Frank was only too delighted to accept, telling the CEO that he knew where the golf club was and would meet them in the club house within the hour. When Frank arrived, the car park was full, so he had to park around the back of the club house. He took his clubs from the boot and joined his company looking forward to a good round of golf.

At the end of a most enjoyable day, the men decided to have dinner in the lounge; Frank agreed saying he would join them presently when he had put his clubs away. At this stage, the car park had emptied considerably and only a few cars were parked around the back of the club house; Frank then noticed Rose's car parked outside the pro shop. He knew that today's tournament was for men only, and Rose never played on this golf course, which intrigued him. As he closed the boot of his car, he saw Rose and the golf pro walking towards the pro shop holding hands; they didn't notice him as they entered the building. For a second, he thought to himself he must be getting a new golf sweater or such like for his upcoming birthday, but he also wondered why would she be buying it here?

As he approached the shop, he noticed the closed sign on the door. Trying the door, he found it was locked so he walked around the side of the building where there was a small window. The blinds were closed but not fully; as he peered inside, he was astonished to see his wife and the pro engaged in intercourse on a display table and Rose seemed to be enjoying herself immensely. Without saying a word, Frank took his phone from his pocket and recorded the whole thing; when he got what he wanted, he rejoined his fellow team mates for dinner.

22

When Sheila returned to the hotel, she was happy to be told that they had availability and she could book in again. On the Monday morning, she headed straight for the restaurant by the sea where she thought she had seen her father. Monday was a much quieter day in the area as there were no markets; determined, Sheila sat there all day people watching. On Tuesday because the market was being held, Sheila arose all the more earlier to make sure she got her seat at the same restaurant with a good vantage point. All morning, she sat there ordering cups of coffee from time to time as the waiters began to whisper about this strange woman. Sheila knew that if she didn't see anyone today, she may as well give up and go home, but for now, all she could do was wait and hope. In the afternoon, the markets were closing up and people were beginning to drift away from the area. Sheila was starting to get disheartened when she heard a voice she recognized coming from the kitchen. It wasn't her father's voice but it was what he was saying that caught her attention...

"Yes yes, ok darlings, I'll see you tomorrow".

When she turned to see who it was, she knew him immediately; it was Bill Vickers the chef sergeant dressed in chef whites whom she had met nearly four years previously in Cyprus. But what was he doing here? She didn't say a word as he passed and as there wasn't much happening, she decided to follow him anyway. He walked up by the closing market and entered the Banco Vistasur. As Sheila waited for Bill to come out again, she wondered to herself, what was Conchita trying to tell her when she said her father's money was withdrawn legally by a Mr Neil Callery-Vickers? But because of GDPR, she could not give her any more information; she was trying to tell her something, but what was it?

When Bill came out again, she followed him and watched as he entered a bar called The Queen Vick with the word QUEEN emblazoned in pride rainbow colours. Outside was a billboard advertising food and free nightly entertainment. The star of the show was none other than Bill Vickers with his promo photo displayed outside; he was dressed in a flamboyant drag outfit. The sign said, "Come one, come all, for a night of fun and frolics". Sheila was intrigued so she decided to come back later that night, get something to eat and watch the show.

When Sheila got back to her room, she lay on her bed trying to put a perspective on things. Joe came into her mind and she wondered if he believed her story about her handbag being stolen at the airport. As she lay there, she considered Joe's proposal; it would mean that she would not have to move away from Stoneybatter, she did like him a lot, maybe even loved him. She knew Joe would love and look after her forever, but in the end, she knew she would never take advantage of such a lovely man and faithful friend just to get a roof over her head. Memories came flooding back of her childhood in Stoneybatter, balaclava's, tank top pullovers, gloves on string through coats, brown leather boots, and the rag and bone man. And Oxmanstown road with its four hundred yellow and red brick terraced town houses, with two hundred on either side. The neighbouring area where there were hundreds of kids playing all sorts of games together and the feeling of belonging to a big loving community where everyone watched out for each other.

The thought of having to move away brought tears to her eyes as she drifted off to sleep, but had fitful dreams where the sheriff and his bailiffs were banging at her barricaded door. As she stood alone behind tables and chairs in the hallway, Rose was shouting through the letter box, "it is my house, so get out". She woke up with a start in darkness and remembered where she was.

Sheila reached the Queen Vick around seven thirty; she took a seat inside with a good view of the stage. It wasn't a very big place, about thirty tables with extra seating outside. The waitress brought her the menu and Sheila ordered a drink as she perused it; she was surprised that she could get a three course meal deal for less than ten euro. For that price, she wasn't expecting much but decided on the tomato soup for starters which was thick and creamy, half roast chicken and chips for the main that came with a fresh side salad, and crème caramel for dessert. When she had finished, she thought to herself, that was a very fine meal and excellent value for money; it was a pity Joan wasn't with her to enjoy it too. She also enjoyed the guitarist playing as the warm-up to the main act.

At 9 pm, a voiceover made an announcement. "Ladies and gentlemen, (and those of you who would desire to transition), would you please put your hands together for our main act of the evening". Followed by a big drum roll. "It's our very own, Queeeen Vick".

The audience went wild clapping and whistling; Sheila looked around at the full house smiling while everyone was cheering as Bill Vickers sashayed onto the stage. She couldn't believe the transformation of this average height, middle aged balding man, who transformed himself into a six foot magnificent vision. He stood in gold platform boots wearing a beautiful dress studded with diamante stones and trimmed with rainbow coloured feathers. Wearing a long red wig, he was plastered in stage makeup and looking every bit a drag queen. Immediately he exploded into his drag act, telling smutty jokes, and singing double-meaning risqué songs. Sheila was surprised at herself laughing and clapping along as everyone was enjoying the show. When it came to his finale, she loved the way he took off his makeup, wig, and clothes bit by bit, to reveal he was indeed a man while singing the song, "I am what I am". At the end of the performance, Sheila, with the rest of the audience stood up to give him a standing ovation. While clapping, Sheila thought to herself, Joan would have loved this.

As people started to leave, Sheila called the waitress for her bill. The waitress returned with her bill and continued to bring the glasses etc into the kitchen through batwing doors. As the doors swung back and forth, Sheila could see into the kitchen just for a split second...

It was then she saw him...

23

Sheila nearly dropped her glass with fright. There was no mistake, she knew it was him; he was busily working away in his chef's whites, and she knew him by the way he moved and his spotless appearance. The waitress remarked to her that she was heading to the wrong door for the ladies' toilet as she walked towards the kitchen but Sheila, as if in a trance, ignored her. Sheila walked into the kitchen and stood in front of the chef saying....

"Hello dad"....

Neil froze at the shock of seeing Sheila standing in front of him, the banging and clattering stopped and the place fell silent as Neil burst out crying. Bill Vickers was in his changing room at the back; he felt the tension and quietness in the air, and he thought the place was being robbed. He burst into the kitchen to see Neil crying and Sheila standing in front of him with all the staff looking on in amazement. Taking control of the situation, he directed the staff to get back to work; he then directed Neil to take Sheila home as they needed privacy and he would finish clearing up. Neil wiping his tears away agreed, so he and Sheila left the restaurant and made the short walk in silence to his apartment.

As soon as Neil closed the door, he turned and hugged Sheila as tightly as he could while kissing her forehead and hair. Sheila, overtaken by his affection, hugged and kissed him back as they both cried while holding each other tightly.

When the moment passed, Neil still holding her hand said gently, "God, Sheila, I've missed you so much".

Sheila replied, "Oh dad, why did you leave me? I never stopped looking for you".

It was then Neil sat Sheila down as he knew he had a lot of explaining to do, but first he wanted to know how she had found him. Sheila explained about Bella Mining Corporation shares while Neil nodded in agreement knowing that he didn't cover his tracks well enough when making the withdrawals. She spoke through tear filled eyes of her six year search for him knowing he was not dead because if he was, she would have felt it in her heart. She told him about the UN Vets and O.N.E. and the support they gave her, and about Mr John Dalton in the little private investigation company in Muckalee Co Kilkenny that was able to trace where the money was withdrawn.

She also told him about how she had travelled to Cyprus and had stood in the kitchen where he had worked; how she had felt his presence there, and then she told him about her breakdown. Sheila didn't say anything about Rose wanting to sell the house when her father was declared legally dead after the seventh year as things had changed drastically now that she had found him. When she had finished speaking, she looked at Neil expectantly waiting for his side of the story.

Neil wiped his eyes and blew his nose in preparation to tell Sheila what she needed to know and why he felt it necessary for him to disappear as he did. Sheila waited for him to speak; as her father looked into her eyes to tell her, the door of the apartment suddenly opened as Bill Vickers entered flamboyantly asking...

"Well darlings, are we all made up now?"

Neil, caught off guard, looked at Bill and then at Sheila; Bill stood in the room looking at the two of them waiting for an answer. Sheila stood up angrily wanting to scratch his eyes out at his intrusion into a very private and important moment when her father was just about to tell her everything she needed to know. She told Bill angrily that he was intruding and it would be better if he left and came back tomorrow. Bill, not knowing what to say, looked open mouthed first at Sheila then at Neil, waiting for him to say something as Sheila stood with her hands on her hips waiting for him to leave.

Eventually, Neil spoke softly saying that Bill couldn't leave because he lived there with him, and Bill was Neil's husband. A silence fell on the room as Sheila tried to comprehend what Neil had just said; as she realized the gravity of the statement, she had to hold the arm of the chair to support herself as she sat down again. Her eyes where wide in disbelief as Neil broke the silence saying that they had got married in Cyprus three years previously. Sheila's head was spinning; she didn't know what to say, and at this point Bill spoke very gently while putting his hand on her shoulder saying, "Darling, we were very much in love".

Sheila angrily brushed his hand away while standing up saying she had to leave now. As she headed for the door, Neil blocked her exit pleading for her not to go as he wanted to tell her everything.

Sheila answered, "Not now, not now, I need some time to take all this in". Neil begged for her to meet him the next day so they could talk again and Sheila agreed as she left.

24

When Sheila got back to her hotel room, she tried to sleep, but sleep wouldn't come; she had a million unanswered questions and thoughts going through her head. The main question being if her father was gay, and was he having a gay relationship while he was married to her mother? She thought of her home life and upbringing, and the fact that her mum and dad were always so loving and caring to each other, she couldn't believe that he would cheat on her.

She remembered how her father would come home from duty in his army greens and the way they would be together in the kitchen, talking and laughing about events of the day, then at an appointed time he would call out to Sheila to get ready for work. He would go upstairs for a shower and afterwards would appear again immaculately turned out in his chef whites ready for their part-time job in the Shelbourne hotel for some function or corporate dinner. Sheila loved working with him as a silver service waitress; she would meet him in the kitchen in her crisp white shirt, black bow tie, black slacks, black shoes highly polished, and white cotton gloves. Her dad, while letting on to be on parade, would inspect her turnout and smile saying, "looking good girl" and Sheila would feel proud as they left for work together.

Then Sheila thought about the last time they had worked together and the circumstances of why she had left her job. Her dad as always was in the kitchen while she was the waitress appointed to look after the bride and groom at the top table of a very prestigious wedding. The bride, or should she be known as "bridezilla" was particularly rude and very demanding with everyone she met, especially to her bridesmaid who seemed to be very nervous but also very attentive to the bride who would snap at her for no reason. The wedding dinner was going fine and everyone seemed to be happy with the meal.

As coffee was served, the best man gave his speech; he then called on the bride and groom to cut the wedding cake. Everyone stood up to clap for the happy couple including the poor unfortunate bridesmaid. Somehow, as she stood up, a full cup of coffee fell from the table spilling all over the front of her lovely pink dress. The bride looked around at her and was furious; she didn't even care if the bridesmaid was scalded or not, she then scolded her in front of everyone. The headwaiter directed Sheila with his eyes to assist her, so Sheila immediately went to her aid and escorted her to the ladies room. When they got inside, Sheila tried to clean the front of the dress as best she could but it was ruined, no matter how she tried there was no way she could get the stain out of the dress for her to return to the table.

Just then the bride burst in to check the damage to the dress ignoring the bridesmaid and Sheila; she never even inquired if she had been burned. When she saw the state of the dress, she turned on the bridesmaid telling her not to bother reappearing back at the table looking like that. She told her to go and change and afterwards when the speeches were over, she could rejoin the wedding; then she stormed out leaving the poor girl in tears. Sheila felt sorry for the girl and introduced herself suggesting they get her cleaned up so she could return to the wedding.

The girl introduced herself as Sandra was saying, "Who wants to return". At this, they both laughed together and made their way upstairs to change.

When inside the bathroom, Sheila filled the bath with warm soapy water to soak the dress and maybe get the coffee stain out. Sandra seemed to be having trouble unzipping the dress at the back, so Sheila said, "Let me help". She opened the hook and eye at the nape of her neck and started unzipping the dress. As she did so and as the zip got lower and lower, Sheila watched as it revealed more of her naked back and became transfixed by her beautiful white skin.

When Sandra turned to thank her, their eyes met in a magical moment as she leaned forward and kissed Sheila on the lips. It was so soft at first but as the kiss was returned, it became more intense as they explored each other's mouths using their tongues. While still in the bathroom, they both removed their clothes, letting them fall to the floor; then naked they made their way to the double bed while fondling, kissing and exploring each other's bodies. Sheila was in ecstasy while Sandra kissed, licked, and caressed her body as she floated towards her first orgasm.

Then to her horror, a voice came from the corner of the room asking, "What is going on here?"

Sheila opened her eyes to see the bride and her mother standing at the open door staring down at the two naked girls. She immediately jumped up trying to hide herself and ran into the bathroom to find her clothes strewn all over the floor while Sandra pulled the bedclothes around herself. As Sheila quickly got dressed, she could hear the bride shouting and causing a scene outside. When she emerged from the bathroom, Sandra was in floods of tears with the bride and her mother standing over her. Without saying a word and totally embarrassed, Sheila began to leave the room but bumped into the hotel manager who looked at her in disgust saying to get her things and go home. Sheila didn't answer him as she retreated down the hallway as quickly as she could.

Outside the hotel, she breathed into her lungs the cool fresh air of the night as she walked aimlessly through the streets of Dublin city trying to understand what just happened and still feeling the touch of Sandra's body next to hers.

She must have been walking for over an hour when her father's car pulled up beside her and he opened the passenger door for her to get in. When she closed the door, Neil turned and asked if she was ok; she didn't answer but nodded yes and they drove home together in silence. When they got home, her mother asked enthusiastically how the wedding went.

Neil spoke, first saying that it wasn't great and they wouldn't be working for that catering company again due to cancellations. Nothing more was said and Sheila smiled at her dad saying she was going to bed as she was tired. The wedding or what happened was never mentioned again, but Sheila would always remember that day in fondness as having the most erotic experience of her life.

25

Early the next morning, Sheila met Neil for breakfast by the seafront; as always it was a beautiful morning with the palm trees waving in the soft warm breeze. As they ate breakfast together, Neil talked while Sheila listened; he assured her that while he was married to her mother Mary, he was totally faithful as she was the love of his life. He told her that after her passing he was lost, distressed, and had even considered suicide; that's when he started going into town alone drinking. It was on such an occasion that he ended up in the George pub (known as a famous Dublin gay bar) where he met an old school pal who was gay. He felt he could talk to him about his loss and how he felt now; after a while, it developed into something more. While coming out of the George one night, he was recognised by a friend of Rose's who told her where she had seen him, so in turn Rose had engaged a private detective to have him followed.

Neil continued, "It was after she came to the house to berate me that I felt I was ruining both your lives. The last thing I wanted to do was to bring shame on the house and my girls, so that night in the house, I promised you I would never hurt you or Rose and formed a plan to get out of your lives forever as you wanted me to".

As Neil was about to continue, Sheila stopped him saying...

"Wait a minute, what do you mean we both wanted, we both wanted what", then she asked the question, "Dad what are you talking about?"

Neil tried to explain about Rose coming over to the house the day Sheila was at work and how she berated him about the company he was keeping. Rose said he could destroy their lives if word got out that he was gay, and they had agreed jointly that he should get out of their lives forever. Sheila remembered her father saying those words in the house years ago; it was after Joe told her about Rose's visit when he heard her shouting at him next door. She thought Rose just wanted to snap him out of his depression and was happy for him when he said, "Things would change for the better".

Sheila began to feel weak; she could feel the blood drain from her body. Neil could also see what was happening as she went pale, and concerned, he called the waiter for a glass of water and a cold compress. As Sheila drank the water, Neil held the compress to the back of her neck and watched as the colour returned to her cheeks. When Sheila regained her composure, she told Neil that she never had that conversation with Rose. She also told him that she never gave up knowing that they would be reunited some day, even in Cyprus when Rose said he was dead.

Neil confessed that he was there when they came looking for him in Cyprus; he said that Bill had come home and pleaded with him to make contact, but he was too afraid as a lot of time had passed. Bill also told him about what had happened in Northern Cyprus and how he and Neil wanted to help by contacting Tommy to offer any bail or legal fees the girls might need, but things worked out ok, and Bill still pleaded with him to reveal himself. But he knew if he was declared legally dead, Sheila and Rose would get the house and any inheritance; he also felt that they were better off without him.

As he spoke, for the first time since they met, Sheila gently took him by the hand saying that when they were in the military kitchen, she felt his presence very strongly and knew she would find him some day. At this, they both leaned over and hugged each other warmly. After breakfast, they decided to walk along the promenade towards Playa de Las Americas; as they walked hand in hand, Sheila realised how well her father was known and liked on the island. As they passed bars and restaurants, waiters and staff would salute or greet him by name with fondness and respect, calling him to stop and have a drink on the house.

As they walked, Neil told her about Bill and how they had met while on duty in Cyprus many years ago as young chefs. He told her that on one of the tours, they decided to buy shares together in the Bella Mining Corporation and make their first million when they struck oil.

He laughed as he said, "But that was only a pipe dream if you'll excuse the pun".

He also told her about the time Bill had won a seat on an RAF flight back to England for Christmas in the camp lottery. As he had no kids and little family, he gave his seat to Neil; Sheila remembered that Christmas and smiled. His face darkened then as he told her how depression taken over him and he had decided to take his own life, but it was Bill who saved him. He told her, on that terrible day, Bill phoned him as he did from time to time, and he knew by the tone of my voice that the black wolf was there.

"Honestly Sheila, I don't know where I would be without him.

He immediately came to Ireland and took me to his home in England at his own expense. Later, he got a posting in Cyprus and that is where we have lived until his retirement three years ago. It was then we decided to get married to avoid any problems with travel documents and passports when we moved to Tenerife, and also the fact that we had fallen in love".

He continued, when Bill took him in as a friend, he was penniless and mentally fragile. He told Sheila how he gave him the strength, support, and the will to go on and how he never intended forming a relationship. But love has a funny way of creeping up on you. It was then Sheila thought to herself, maybe she had been a little harsh with Bill Vickers as now she was seeing another side to him.

26

They had walked a lot further than they thought and decided to stop for lunch in Porto Colon.

Neil told her it was then they decided to take the money from what was left of Bella Mining Corporation to use as a deposit on the Queen Vick. As they were using Bill's surname, they never thought their withdrawal could be traced back to them as they both had a fifty/fifty share. Neil felt that it was also his way of contributing to the business they had set up together. It was then Neil said how sorry he was for leaving them both, but felt at the time and under the circumstances, it was best for everyone. He also said he was very disappointed at how Rose was treating Sheila with regard to selling the house from under her and making her homeless; especially since she had a big house in Castleknock and was doing so well for herself. Sheila told Neil how good Joe was to her, even to the point of proposing to her so she wouldn't move away. Neil said he knew Joe would want to look after her as he always loved her, but never had the bottle to say it.

Then he said, "He is a good sort Joe, with a good heart and would make some girl happy, but not you".

Sheila was surprised at Neil's statement; she was going to ask him what he meant by it, but decided to let it go for now.

As the afternoon turned into evening, they decided to get a taxi back to Los Christianos. When they approached the Queen Vick, Sheila recognised the bank manager Conchita Martinez and Bill Vickers sitting out on the veranda in the evening sun having a drink together. She could see the delight on Bill's face when he saw they were holding hands; he stood up smiling ushering them to their table where Conchita was sitting as introductions were made. Smiling broadly, Conchita said they had already met and leaned across to kiss Sheila on the cheek which made her blush. When they were all seated, Bill got the drinks while noisily saying how happy he was that Sheila was here with them.

As it transpired, the day Sheila left the bank having told her story to Conchita, she contacted Bill. Conchita wanted to tell Neil immediately about Sheila looking for him, but Bill told her that he tried and failed to bring them together in Cyprus. He felt it might cause his depression to return and make him run away again. So they both decided to wait and see what the bank's legal department had to say about GDPR as to what information Conchita could impart to Sheila about her father. If everything failed, Bill said at least Neil would be happy not knowing about Sheila and at the end of the day, all that mattered to Bill was Neil's happiness.

When the legal department gave their instruction not to break protocol on GDPR, Conchita was devastated for Sheila, and that is why she hinted to her about the man with the Irish accent. But nobody expected that Sheila would spot her father leaving the restaurant after his breakfast shift on that Sunday morning, and that she would be staying on in Tenerife to look for him which put the whole process in motion.

As it was getting late, Bill made an announcement that he had to get ready for his show that night as he gaily threw back his head saying, "My public deserve me darlings". They all smiled at this and Neil said he needed to prepare the kitchen also. Sheila said she would come back later to see the show; at this Conchita asked her if she would like some company. Sheila immediately agreed and a table was reserved for them both. When Sheila got back to her room, her mind was racing with all the information she received during the day. As she showered, she could not take her mind off Conchita and the way she had kissed her so softly on the cheek, which made her blush again.

That evening, Sheila was first to arrive at the Queen Vick and ordered a drink while waiting for Conchita to arrive; her dad popped his head out of the kitchen and waved at her, she smiled back at him and blew him a kiss. Sheila couldn't contain her excitement waiting for Conchita; she felt like a child waiting in a queue to see Santa, instead of a grown woman meeting a friend. When she arrived, Sheila's heart skipped a beat; she had to take a second look at how she was dressed. Instead of a sophisticated bank manager in a pencil suit, there stood a beautiful vision wearing a T shirt tucked into body hugging jeans with elegant beaded sandals. Her hair hung loosely to her shoulders and was held back by designer sun glasses perched on her head. She looked absolutely stunning and Sheila told her so as she moved in to let her sit down, which earned her a big smile and a kiss on the cheek.

27

That night Sheila had the best time she could ever remember; the food that was sent to the table by her father plus the company of Conchita was second to none, even Bill's show was better the second time around. Afterwards, when everyone had gone, they just sat talking and drinking into the early hours of the morning. When the night was over, Neil said he would walk Sheila to her apartment, but Conchita insisted on walking her as it was on the way to her house anyway. The night was warm and magical as the two girls walked and chatted as if they had known each other for years. When they reached Sheila's apartment, Conchita went to kiss her on the cheek good night, but instead gently kissed her on the lips. As they embraced and kissed again, Sheila melted into Conchita's arms. Her heart was pounding so hard in her chest she thought it would burst, and then without saying another word, Sheila led Conchita by the hand to her apartment.

The next morning, Sheila woke to the sound of the breeze softly lifting the curtains on her window as the dappled sunlight shone through them. She turned on her pillow to see Conchita sleeping beside her and thought to herself, I must be in heaven as joy filled her heart. She was afraid to move in case the moment would end, but Conchita opened her eyes and smiled at her while putting out her hand to embrace her.

Later, as Conchita was showering, there was a knock on the door; Sheila opened it thinking it was the maid, but she was astonished to see Rose standing there. Without saying a word, Rose went to step inside the apartment but Sheila blocked her entrance; Rose looked up in surprise as Sheila said she was busy at the moment and would see her later.

Rose didn't move but tried to look past Sheila to peer into the apartment while asking her, "What's going on, have you someone in there?"

Sheila, more assertive this time, blocked her vision while saying, "I told you I would meet you later".

Sheila felt that this time she was not running away as she did at the wedding, and she would not be looked at as if she was dirty and did something wrong. What happened last night was beautiful and nobody was going to mar her beautiful experience. Rose was taken aback at Sheila's new found strength and decided not to force the issue; she told her the number of her apartment and walked away without saying another word. As Sheila closed the door smiling to herself, she knew that NOBODY would ever make her feel less than she was again.

Sheila's heart skipped a beat as Conchita emerged from the shower naked, casually drying her hair with a towel. She couldn't believe that a woman as beautiful as her would have any interest in a girl who wore dark frumpy clothes to hide her appearance. Conchita saw Sheila looking at her body; smiling she walked over to her and kissed her softly on the mouth whispering to her how beautiful she looked in the morning sun. Sheila's heart just soared with delight while returning her kiss.

Later Sheila explained about Rose's visit and that she would have to meet her; this concerned Conchita and she offered to go along with her so she wouldn't be intimidated by her. Sheila declined gratefully saying that the time had come when she had to stand up for herself and sort out some family business that was well over due, but she did ask Conchita not to say anything to her father or Bill as she needed to straighten some things out with Rose first.

28

It was well into the afternoon before Sheila decided to find Rose after promising Conchita she would contact her later. When she went to the pool area it was easy enough to find Rose; as usual she was sitting at the bar chatting up a young bartender smiling and flirting. As Sheila approached, Rose saw her and said sarcastically, "You took your time".

Sheila ignoring the remark said, "Do you want to talk or not?"

Rose replied, "Why can't we talk here?"

Sheila said, "What we have to talk about should be said in private, so make up your mind, your place or mine?" Surprised at Sheila's attitude, Rose agreed they should go to her apartment as she wanted to change her clothes anyway. There wasn't a word spoken as the two girls walked to the apartment, but as soon as the door was closed, Sheila turned to Rose wanting to know how she found out she was here.

Rose replied in her usual assertive voice that she knew those two fucking eejit's (meaning Frank and Joe) were up to something; the two of them couldn't organise a piss up in a brewery. Sneeringly, Rose said that she had known Sheila was in Tenerife because wimpy Joe had contacted her all worried that you were having another breakdown. She started to laugh as she told her, "The two fools thought they were going to organise a "rescue mission" where Joe would come here all alone and bring you home and I wouldn't find out about it". She said, "All they had to do was to contact Joan, your travel companion and they would have known you were ok; anyway I got the two of them together and told them "what for", which put an end to their stupid little scheme".

As Sheila listened, she was touched that Joe and Frank thought so much of her that they would want to make sure she was ok. Especially Joe, that he was so gallant to travel outside Ireland alone to save her; she thought how lucky she was to have such a good friend to depend on.

Rose interrupted her thoughts saying... "Well, what about you, what the fuck are you doing here, and who did you have in your apartment this morning? Some fucking toy boy waiter you met when you were with Joan; you had a holiday romance and fell in love, I'd bet".

Sheila retorted saying that it was none of her business who she had in her apartment, and furthermore, the reason she was in Tenerife was to find her father.

Before she could finish, Rose exploded angrily while shouting into her face... "For fuck's sake Sheila, not this again. I thought we had put that to bed in Cyprus four years ago; anyway we don't have to sell the house now.

Frank wants a divorce and I have agreed, so I will be moving back in with you".

Sheila was dumb struck as Rose ranted on, "That fucking asshole, Frank, after all I have done for him. If I hadn't waited for two hours in the freezing cold on that fucking bridge over the Liffey, he would never be where he is today. I got him to move out of that stupid bachelor flat and move to Castleknock where he would be noticed as a 'high achiever'. I pushed and pushed him to assert himself in the company until he was where he is today, and with me by his side, we were known as the perfect couple. Now the fucking fool wants to throw it all away over some stupid indiscretion he found out about and said he has film to prove it. Honestly, I don't know how he acquired the film, he must have had me followed or something like that".

Sheila thought to herself, good for you Frank, it was a long time coming.

When Rose had finished her rant and the room fell quiet, she said ever so softly, more like a whisper... "Rose, I've found dad".

29

You could have heard a pin drop; the blood drained from Rose's face as she sat with her mouth open, absolutely speechless. Minutes passed between them as Rose digested the statement; her eyes filled and tears began to roll down her cheek; eventually she asked… "Where is he?"

It was then that Sheila's anger began to rise as she said to Rose, "Never mind where he is. It's WHY he felt he had to run away from us, I want to know". WHY, when he was at his lowest point emotionally that he felt he had nobody to turn to for help and understanding of what he was going through?"

She continued, "WHY was he cast out from our little family because he felt he would embarrass or bring down shame on our so called, good name in the community? BUT, really, what I want to know is… WHO put this insane idea into his head in the first place, something I had no input into whatsoever?"

Sheila watched Rose's face lower in acknowledgement to her questions as tears rolled down her cheeks; she had to grip both sides of the armchair she was sitting in until her knuckles went white. She wanted to jump forward and tear both sides of Rose's face with her nails but somehow kept her control as she waited for her answers. The scene was charged with emotion and Sheila was ready to pounce on Rose if she uttered one wrong word. Eventually, Rose lifted her head to look at Sheila wiping her face and blowing her nose, then her expression changed from sorrow to anger as she sobbed out the words Sheila could not believe she was hearing.

"It was always the two of you, yes, always you and him, working together, talking together, you, daddy's little girl always getting his attention. BUT WHAT ABOUT ME, WHAT PRAISE DID I GET?"

Rose continued, "I had to work for everything I had, nobody seemed to care or acknowledge what I had achieved, and when mam died, it was all just perfect. You two would live together and carry on in your own blissful relationship, but WHO cared about me and how I felt? Especially when I was told by my friend that my father was carrying on in some fucking gay bar with some other fucking queer."

"WHAT ABOUT ME!!!"

"What about my reputation and how I would feel if it got out in my circle of friends or corporate business associates? I had to contain this as quickly as possible. When I spoke to dad that day, I told him in no uncertain terms what his carrying on would do to us but I didn't think he would disappear as he did. I thought he would just cop himself on, then, after he disappeared, I thought he would just come home when he was ready asking for our forgiveness. Of course as the years passed, I did believe he was dead and as far as I was concerned, I was entitled to half his estate just as you were even if you were his favourite little daddy's girl".

Sheila had heard enough; without even thinking, she lunged forward slapping Rose hard in the face. She turned her hands into claws scratching both sides of her face with her nails. As the two girls fought, they fell over a coffee table, both banging their heads on the tiled floor, almost knocking each other out. Sheila got up from the floor as if in slow motion, stunned from the knock to her head. She looked down at her hand to see her broken finger nails and a fist full of blond hair entangled in her fingers.

As her senses returned, she turned to see Rose getting up off the floor to clean herself up. Sheila didn't say a word as she threw the matted hair on the floor and walked out the door. When Sheila reached the lobby of the apartment block, she started to fall apart; while standing there shaking and sobbing, she heard a familiar voice call her name. Turning to see who it was, she couldn't believe her eyes to see Joe standing there smiling at her.

Sheila ran to him, wrapping her arms tightly around his neck; after a moment, she stood back to see if it was really him. As she saw the look of concern on Joe's face, she looked up to see her reflection in the hall mirror of a very dishevelled person looking back and hugged Joe again all the tighter.

Joe said, "My god Sheila, who did this to you?"

But Sheila just smiled at Joe, happy to see him saying, "Now don't start worrying, I'm fine Joe, honestly, but you should see the other fellow". Then they walked back to her apartment together.

30

As Sheila cleaned herself up in the bathroom, Joe explained how Rose had found out about their plan to come and help her if she was in trouble; they knew Rose was not happy with their interference but they had decided to go ahead with it anyway. He couldn't believe it when Sheila while laughing told him that Rose and she had already met, referring to her dishevelled state saying, "That was the result of our meeting", then she said, "She had it coming for a long time and it felt great".

When Sheila came out of the bathroom with her hair washed and smiling from ear to ear, Joe fell in love with her all over again. Suddenly she pulled him out of his chair saying "Come on, let's go for a drink, there's loads to talk about, and I want you to meet a friend of mine I think you'll know".

Joe felt elated as he knew that Sheila was fine while watching her as they walked in the sunshine to the Queen Vick Bar. When they were seated, Sheila called over Bill who Joe thought was a waiter; she ordered a bottle of champagne and four glasses while asking Bill, "Is he inside?"

When Bill confirmed that he was, Joe was a little confused at their behaviour but said nothing. When the drinks were served, Bill sat down beside Joe smiling, then Sheila left the table and skipped over into the kitchen as Joe watched in anticipation as to what was going to happen next. Then Sheila emerged again and Joe saw Neil standing by her side; he broke down crying but smiling at the same time. They all came together smiling and hugging as Sheila explained to Joe what Bill was to her father and how happy she was at this moment.

A couple of days later, when Sheila had cooled off, she went around to Rose's apartment to apologise for her outburst. She hoped they could put the past behind them and maybe move forward again as a family, but Rose had already checked out and returned to Ireland.

When Rose got home from Tenerife, she found the house empty of all Frank's belongings. On the dining room table was a letter from Frank saying he had enough of her bullying and downright bad behaviour. He said that while she was away, he had gotten further evidence of her many infidelities with times and dates supplied by his private investigator. They were lodged and filed with his solicitor, especially the video of her having sex on the table in the golf club. He went on to say if she agreed to the divorce quickly and amicably, ALL evidence found would be destroyed. Also, as they had no children or complications in their sham of a marriage, they could split everything fifty, fifty and just get on with their lives without hurting each other any further.

When Rose had finished reading the letter she opened her phone and played back the video; realizing it was Frank who recorded it, she closed her phone again and cried in shame. She knew Frank was a decent man and he didn't deserve the way she had behaved or treated him. As she put her phone back in the bag, she decided that she would stop hurting the people she loved and turn over a new leaf.

But as Rose sat alone in her big house in Castleknock having driven her husband and whole family away, she stood and looked at her reflection in the mirror. She turned her head slightly to see a bald patch at the side where Sheila had pulled out her hair and the scratches on her face, as she touched it lightly with her finger tips she knew there were no more leaves to turn over, and she had come to the end of the book.

31

As Joe walked along the promenade with the sun on his face wearing shorts, T shirt, and sandals that Sheila had bought him in the market he felt very pleased with himself. They felt very different from the black leather shoes, corduroy trousers, long sleeved shirt, pullover, and padded coat he had brought with him. As he walked alone, he listened to the waves of the Atlantic Ocean gently lapping on the seashore. He watched as the palm trees waved in the gentle breeze and marvelled at the beautiful colours of the bougainvillea cascading over fences and walls as he strolled.

His thoughts turned to Sheila and how happy she was here; how she had laughed at him dripping with perspiration in all his winter clothing and how he loved her more with each passing day. It was on one of those days while he sat with Sheila outside the Queen Vick having a cool beer in the sunshine, he was introduced to a very elegant lady called Conchita.

When they first met, he didn't really notice anything out of the ordinary when they greeted each other with a kiss on the cheek. But as the conversation continued, he began to notice how animated Sheila became in her presence. It wasn't very noticeable in the beginning, but it was in the way they spoke to each other smiling, touching, holding hands, and looking into each other's eyes. Joe didn't feel left out of the conversation or anything like that, but somehow he felt a little bit like an intruder. Although Conchita was lovely to him, she made Joe feel very relaxed in their company as they teased him for saying he was burning up in his totally unsuitable winter clothing.

As he strolled, his thoughts turned to home and how around this time, he would be sitting alone by the fireside. He would be holding a cup of hot tea in his hand, wondering what he would prepare for his evening meal before getting ready for his night shift, and thought to himself smiling, this is the life I should be living.

He had contacted Frank and given him a full report on Sheila; he also told him about Neil and his new marital status. He filled him in about Bill Vickers and the Queen Vick; he also mentioned Rose had returned to Ireland without making contact with either Sheila, or Neil. Frank thanked Joe for the update; he said he was delighted for them now that they were together again. He said that he was especially happy for Sheila as she never gave up on finding her dad. He told Joe not to worry about Rose as he had things in hand; before he hung up, he told him to stay on and enjoy his time in Tenerife and not to worry about the expense as he had it covered.

It was coming towards the end of the second week and Joe was thinking about his flight home when his phone rang. Frank was on the other end and sounded concerned; he told Joe that Rose had tried to take her own life. She was in hospital in intensive care; they had her in an induced coma and the prognosis was very bad. The hospital had contacted him as he was listed as the next of kin; they suggested that the family should be contacted and be prepared for the worst as Rose was failing. He also wanted Joe to convey the bad news to Sheila and Neil personally as they needed to be told immediately.

When Sheila, Neil and Bill arrived at Dublin airport, Frank was waiting to drive them straight to the hospital. He told them what happened to Rose and how she was found by the cleaner, having left her mobile phone in the kitchen; she rang it continually knowing Rose was in the house. After getting no answer, she decided to return and retrieve it about an hour later. As she had a key, she let herself in and hearing loud music upstairs, she called up to Rose saying she had only come back for her phone. When she got no reply, a bad feeling came over her so she went upstairs to investigate.

She found Rose sitting in the bath tub in a pool of blood with a bottle of vodka beside her. She immediately called for an ambulance but by the time it arrived, her pulse was very low from a massive loss of blood. The medical team tried everything including four blood transfusions, but she was not responding and was failing fast.

It was suggested to Frank that he contact her immediate family to come to say their last goodbyes and to give their consent to have the life support system switched off if her condition continued to deteriorate.

As they entered Rose's room, the hospital Chaplain was just finishing administering the last rights as he anointed her. A nurse was standing by her bedside checking her pulse, she smiled sadly at them saying she was resting now and indicated she would leave, but would come back later to see if they needed anything. The only sound in the room was the ventilator pumping air into her lungs, and the monitor beeping softly in the background.

Sheila and Neil sat beside her bed, gently taking her hand saying their little family was reunited as they asked Rose not to leave them. They spent the whole night with her while Frank and Bill waited in the family room giving them privacy to say their goodbyes to Rose.

Two days later, Joe arrived back in Ireland; he was surprised when Frank picked him up from the airport to be told that Rose hadn't passed but was still critical. Frank told him that Sheila and Neil had not left her bedside since arriving home and were exhausted but nothing Bill or Frank said would convince them to leave her.

It was a further three weeks before Rose opened her eyes to see them still sitting beside her bed. As she looked around and feeling very weak she was unable to talk, Sheila was holding her hand while her father stood behind her smiling and saying to Rose that she would be alright now, thank God. Slowly she drifted off to sleep again.

While sleeping she dreamt her mother had come to her bedside frequently to hold her hand; while she was with her, they would talk and laugh together about old times when Rose was growing up. Her mother Mary told her of how strong she was in body and soul and that although she was feeling very weak at this moment, her strength would return so she could help her father and little sister Sheila whose hearts were breaking. She told her that their little family was growing and they would need someone strong to be able to guide them to a successful future as a loving unit.

Rose asked Mary how she could guide the family as she had tried and succeeded in pulling them apart as well as her own marriage that she had destroyed. But Mary held her hand all the tighter while smiling and saying, "Love has a way of finding a route through anything, but it needs time and strength and you have both in abundance". Mary told her then that she would have to leave her now but would be with her always as she found her way. As Mary started to drift away, Rose became agitated and begged Mary not to leave her but as she did, her eyes flickered open to see Sheila still holding her hand as before. Rose smiled at Sheila as she drifted off to a restful sleep again knowing she was loved.

It was later that night, Rose woke again to see her father sitting beside her still holding her hand softly. Tears welled up in her eyes as she tried to say to him dryly that she was so sorry for all the hurt she had caused.

Neil tut-tutted as he calmed his daughter saying to rest now as everything would be alright and just get better so she could go home to her loving family. As Rose sleepily drifted off again, she said to Neil that she had no family to go home to as she destroyed everything she touched as she was toxic. Again Neil, rubbing the back of her hand, shushed her as he told her it was not true but Rose didn't hear him as she slept. In her dreams again, Mary returned and Rose asked her was she there to take her home? Mary said no as it was not her time; she told Rose that she had a long and loving life to lead with children to rear as well as guiding her large family. Rose was confused and asked Mary how could that be? But Mary calmed her daughter saying again to let love find its way and she would be fine as she drifted away again leaving Rose calling out to her not to go.

As she was calling out to her mother, she felt the soothing soft hand of someone calmly stroking her forehead while talking gently to her. When she opened her eyes to see who it was, she saw Frank standing over her looking down lovingly. As she recognised him, she started to cry while telling him how sorry she was, but Frank kissed her softly on her forehead again and told her not to worry and just get better so she could come back to him because he still loved her dearly. So Rose closed her eyes again and drifted off into a restful sleep.

32

Rose spent another week in the intensive care ward before being moved to a step-down facility.

Psychiatric, counselling professionals, as well as a close family loving unit, took over to help Rose recover and regain her mental wellbeing and strength. It was a further three weeks before Rose was discharged and went home to Castleknock. Frank had prepared everything for her return. It was also arranged that Sheila would move into the house and would work in Tommy O Gara's as normal but would be available for Rose when she was off duty. Frank moved back in but had a room next to Rose; they wanted to see if they could rekindle their love through marriage counselling while receiving medical counseling, which Rose still needed. Neil returned to Tenerife to run the Queen Vick with Bill but he also had a spare room put aside for him so he could return every chance he got to visit his girls.

Over the following months, Rose regained her strength and while having a cup of coffee one morning with Sheila, she told her about their mother's visits when she was in hospital. She said that mam had told her that her family was growing and that her strength and guidance would be needed, but she was confused as to what she meant by that? She asked Sheila if she could put some perspective on what she was trying to tell her. Sheila, feeling very uncomfortable as to what Rose was talking about but not wanting to agitate Rose in any way, tried to approach the question sensitively knowing that it might have been the high dosage of medication she was on. So trying to appease her sister as best she could, she said maybe their mother was trying to say that our little family was getting bigger with the marriage of their father and Bill.

She laughed out loud as she said, "I hope they weren't going to have a baby".

At this, the two girls laughed together; Sheila then relaxed feeling that she had answered Rose's question sensitively. Then Rose said that maybe mam was preparing her for the news that dad had married a man and she was happy for them both; at this Sheila shook her head in agreement and the two girls held hands in companionable silence in their own thoughts.

33

Over the next few months, life returned to normal, or what normal should have been. Frank and Rose continued their marriage counselling and decided that Frank should move back in to the same room. Rose rejoined the gym but gave up golfing; they seemed so happy again that Sheila decided to move back to Stoneybatter. Sheila was very happy to be back in her own home as it meant she could invite Conchita over for weekends as they were missing each other so much only keeping in contact by zoom calls. Conchita would also keep her up to date on the Queen Vick as she was also missing her dad but she was happy to learn that the business was doing very well.

Joe went back to his night security job in Grange Gorman, coming home every morning as before, tired and cold while thinking to himself about what he would be having for his evening meal alone before going up to bed with a hot cup of tea in his hand and wishing he was back in Tenerife, lying in the sun with a cool beer. But he was especially delighted when Sheila moved back home as he had missed her dreadfully; the first thing he did was to invite her in for one of their chats and a meal together. Also while Neil would be visiting, he would stay with Sheila and it sort of felt like old times joining him for a pint while Sheila was working in the pub. But then he thought, things will never go back to old times because he worried, as Joe always worried about the future, as to what would happen if Sheila decided to move away and live with Conchita in Tenerife. He knew he would be happy for her, but he also knew that it would kill him.

But Joe needn't have worried because only six months later Neil and Bill contacted everyone saying that they wanted to hold a family meeting in Dublin. Frank and Rose were asked to provide the venue for the meeting that would be held in their house in Castleknock. It was arranged that Neil, Bill, and Conchita would arrive in Dublin the night before and Conchita would stay with Sheila. Conchita would not reveal to her what the meeting was about no matter how much Sheila tried to extract the information from her. Conchita would just kiss her on the cheek saying she would just have to wait and see like all the others. Neil and Bill would stay in Castleknock with Frank and Rose. Nobody knew what this Family announcement was going to be and everyone was making assumptions.

Rose all excited as to what was going to be announced, asked Sheila jokingly, "Do you think Neil and Bill are having a baby", and the two girls burst out laughing together at the thought of it. Joe called into Sheila again worried that he had received an invitation as he felt it might have been sent to the wrong person.

But Sheila in turn asked Joe. "Why wouldn't you re-
ceive an invitation as you are part of our family?" Which
made Joe smile broadly.

34

As they all gathered in Frank and Rose's sitting room waiting patiently on the evening of the meeting there was great anticipation as to what the announcement would be. Eventually, Bill Vickers opened his brief case taking out seven A4 manila folders with each person's name on the front. He handed them around the room while asking them not to open the file until he and Neil explained the contents and what the meeting was about.

Then Bill started his speech; he told them that the Queen Vick in Tenerife was going from strength to strength and they have now realized that the premises they have was getting too small for the nightly custom they were getting. So after careful consideration, Neil and Bill had decided to expand and open second premises in the upmarket area of Fanabe in the Costa Adeje area of Playa De Las Americas. He continued, but to achieve this business plan of expansion and as Neil and Bill were getting a little older, as he said with a sniff while tipping his eye brows flamboyantly, they would need an investment package. To get them started, they wanted to get much larger premises that they already had viewed and reserved temporarily, then Bill looked at Neil and asked him to take over as he sat down. Neil stood up and carried on; he told them that the entertainment and restaurant part of the business would be no problem to run as Neil and Bill could prove from the success of the Queen Vick 1. But to really make this venture foolproof, they would need to engage a young and dynamic team of professionals who would be offered a partnership to help the business succeed. Then he asked as he pointed to each person seated in the room...

"Who better to offer this partnership to, other than your own family?"

At this stage, everyone looked at each other confused but Neil carried on speaking. He told them, "In front of you in the manila folder is our business plan and the role we think will suit your specific areas of expertise. We have also included ways of how each individual would be able to make a monetary investment into the venture. The investment required would not be too much as we would only be needing start up cash to begin with to cover rent, and refurbishment of the premises etc. We have already received a line of credit from Conchita's bank which is the Banco Vistasur Canarias in Los Christianos where we hold our accounts".

Neil finished off by saying that they did not have to give them an answer immediately but asked them to give the business proposal careful consideration and if they had any questions or concerns to come back to them. As the meeting was ending, Rose stood up and said that as all the family was together at this moment, she and Frank would like to make an announcement of their own. As Rose took Frank's hand in hers smiling, she said that she was three months pregnant and they were both delighted to share their joy with them all tonight. At that moment, everyone in the room congratulated them both especially Neil and Sheila who hugged and kissed Rose.

Sheila then whispered while winking at Rose...

"Maybe mam was right about our family expanding after all".

Rose while smiling said, "I know, and I feel her presence with me even now".

That night when everyone had gone from the meeting, Frank and Rose lay in each other's arms. They discussed how they could manage to go forward with Neil and Bill's proposal; also how it might affect their young and growing family going forward into the future. Frank could not see any problem with his position as financial controller of the Queen Vick 2 as he was already working from home in his present position in the financial services sector. He knew he would only have to check the books on a quarterly basis which wouldn't be a problem for him.

Rose on the other hand was worried that now, after all the trouble and hurt she had caused in her family and especially to Frank. Rose didn't want to jeopardise their new found love and affection for each other by moving away from Castleknock. Frank assured her that nothing would ever come between their love for each other again as they hugged and kissed. He then said that maybe this opportunity being offered to her was what she needed to give her a purpose in going forward. He continued, and besides even if the whole venture fell flat on its face, once they were together like this, they could overcome any obstacle. As they lay in agreement together, they both drifted off to sleep.

As Rose slept, she dreamt her mother Mary came to her; Rose was delighted she had returned. She excitedly told her mother of how she was right in saying that "love would find a way in her recovery"; she said how happy she was in soul and body now that she was pregnant. She also said that now her family were reconciled, they could move on to this new and exciting venture together. Mary seemed happy as Rose spoke to her about her redemption, but warned her that maybe she had not reconciled with all of her family which could jeopardise their happiness in the future. Rose was confused; she asked Mary who else she could have hurt when she was so bitter before. But Mary replied as she drifted away to look deeper into her soul as all was not as it seemed in her growing family.

Rose called on Mary again and again to come back, but Mary had left and Frank was holding her in his arms as she woke; he said she must have a bad dream and was calling out. As Rose lay back down on her pillow, sleep would not come as she pondered her dream.

35

Two weeks later when Neil and Bill returned to find out if everyone was in agreement with their plan of expansion and to answer any questions they might have, everyone was in agreement in forming the partnership except Joe. In withdrawing, Joe said in his own words, that at this time in his life, he felt that the plan was not for him. Although, he said with a little sadness in his voice, he wished them all every success and happiness going forward in their future together.

The room fell silent as everyone looked at Joe in disappointment, but they respected his decision all the same. Sheila was devastated; she couldn't believe he was pulling out after all the conversations they had about how much he loved Tenerife and how he would love to live there.

Later, after the meeting had ended, Sheila confronted Joe about this asking him what changed his mind? But Joe sadly told her that after careful consideration, he felt that, at this time of life and with a secure job and home of his own, moving to Tenerife just didn't feel right for him and his decision was final. Sheila knew that Joe had made up his mind and there was no convincing him otherwise, but wondered what had brought him to his decision as she felt he was making a terrible mistake. Afterwards when Joe had gone home alone, Sheila conveyed her worries to everyone hoping that somehow they might be able to convince him to change his mind. But everyone was lost for words as to what they could say.

When Joe got home, he put on the kettle for a cup of tea, as he sat down at the kitchen table he banged his fist hard shaking everything on top...

Joe was angry...

He was angry with himself...

He was angry with his decision...

He was angry with the whole Callery family... But above all, he was angry with Sheila...

He tried to rationalise his anger but he couldn't. He thought to himself, how could Sheila be so cruel to him in rejecting his proposal of marriage? And then to take up with Conchita knowing it would break his heart. He thought about when Conchita would visit Sheila; as he lay in bed at night he could hear their sounds of love-making through the wall next door which frustrated him even more. Then he thought about Neil and Bill and how happy and successful they were together, but he was angry at Neil for the six years of worry he had caused to Sheila and him for disappearing. In his anger he thought, and now there was Neil with his new life and partner while Joe stayed at home with no future while the only love of his life was moving away...

Then his anger turned to another Callery... ROSE...

That foul mouthed bitch who made everyone's life a misery, and caused all the trouble in the Callery household by driving Neil away in the first place. Everyone forgave her for the terrible hurt and trouble she caused by faking her own suicide, then she comes out of it all sugar coated and playing happy families. But Joe would never forgive her, for Joe knew what a total vindictive little tramp she was.

36

He recalled that during the meeting at their house in Castleknock Joe went upstairs to use the toilet, nobody noticed Rose following him. As Joe came out, Rose was standing outside waiting; as he passed Rose asked him, what did he think about Neil and Bill's plan? Joe replied that he loved the idea and couldn't wait to get the family business up and running; he also told her he was looking forward to the challenge of his new position in the company. Then Rose retorted sneeringly...

"But you are not family, are you?" As she smiled at him and closed the toilet door, Joe was left standing in the hallway alone with his thoughts totally shocked to the core.

Over the next six months, Joe saw less and less of Sheila as plans progressed in Tenerife getting closer to the opening of Queen Vick 2. He was getting used to the idea of Sheila not living next door and carried on as normal. Even when Sheila came home, she would phone or text him for a meet-up and chat, but Joe would always give her an excuse that he had already made plans or was working.

It was around this time, Joe opened his hall door to a knock. He was astonished to see Rose standing outside holding a baby in her arms. He was dumbstruck at first; so Rose broke the silence asking if she could come inside. Joe didn't know what to say so he stood aside and let her in. Joe showed Rose into the sitting room as he didn't intend making her comfortable by offering her a cup of tea or anything else. When they were seated, Joe waited expectantly to hear what Rose had to say. Rose realizing this decided she would speak first and get to the point of her visit as she could feel the tension in the room. First of all, Rose held up her sleeping baby for Joe to see and introduced her as Mary the same name as her mother. This broke the ice a little and Joe congratulated Rose and Frank... The silence returned...

So Rose explained she was around in the Church of the Sacred Heart to book Mary's christening; she told him that was the reason she was in the area and had decided to call and see him. Joe nodded but said nothing still waiting to find out why she called. Rose still trying to break the tension said while smiling weakly...

"That was where we were christened as well Joe. You, me, and Sheila. They were good days back then when we were all together and time has passed so quickly".

Joe smiled back at Rose a little and nodded in agreement. But having enough of Rose's chit-chat and expecting some sort of knock-back from her, Joe decided to ask the obvious question while agreeing they were good days but...

"Why are you here Rose?"...

Rose realizing her pleasantries with Joe were not working decided to get to the point of the real reason she had called. But just before she spoke, in her mind she had a flash-back. Six months previously, she dreamed her mother had visited her saying that Rose should look deeper in to her soul to reunite her family. As the months of her pregnancy slowly passed, Rose reflected on how badly she had treated Joe and remembered all those terrible things she had said to him over the years.

Then Rose began speaking again saying the real reason she had called to see him was to apologise for all the hurt she had caused him over the years. She said all her stupid snide remarks succeeded in driving him away from their family, but in doing so it has left a big empty void in their lives that cannot be filled without him. She continued, as their family moved forward together, there was always someone missing and because of that, their new venture felt pointless somehow. She asked Joe if there was any chance that maybe, he might be able to put those terrible things she had said behind him and forgive her as a brother because she felt while growing up, Joe was more of a brother to her than a next door neighbour. She continued, on reflection she had realized how strong Joe was in defying her when Sheila was on her own in Tenerife and going so far out of his comfort zone to try and help her. She told him only a man with his strength of character would be able to follow true on what he felt was the right thing to do. She also said he was a true and loyal friend to all of their family who was sadly missed from their circle. When Rose finished speaking, Joe feeling more at ease, thanked her for her unusually kind words.

Then Rose smiled at Joe saying there was just one more favour she needed to ask him before she left...

Joe tensed up and waited for her Knock-back...

Rose told Joe that she and Frank had talked. They wanted to know if he would consider being Mary's God father as they both agreed there would not be a more up-standing person than him for the role.

As Rose slept that night, she dreamed her mother Mary returned to her, but saying nothing she just smiled at her nodding her head before disappearing forever. Rose slept soundly that night, for the first time in years.

37

In the military church of the Sacred Heart, Arbour Hill, Joe stood beside Sheila at the water font as Mary's Godparents. As Joe looked into Sheila's eyes he wished it had been their baby that was being christened that day and not Rose and Frank's. But in his heart, he now knew that his dream was never to be. He looked across the aisle to see Conchita sitting in the front row looking very elegant and beautiful and thought to himself how happy she makes Sheila feel and obviously how much in love they seem.

After the ceremony, the whole family went back to the Castleknock golf and country club for lunch, which was more like a wedding reception than a christening ceremony as Rose had arranged every detail to the last. When coffee was being served, Rose and Frank were called upon to say a few words to mark the occasion. Everyone banged their hands on the table in agreement. It was Rose who stood up to say how happy they were to be blessed with such a beautiful little girl and how happy they both were to have all the family together at one table to celebrate with. She thanked her sister Sheila and her adopted brother Joe for standing up to the task of

Godparents to Mary and knows how lucky she is to have them in her life. But not to forget to buy her birthday and Christmas presents every year for the rest of her life, as everyone banged on the table again laughing as well as Joe. Then Rose said earnestly that as the family moved closer to their new venture together in Tenerife, she hoped Joe might reconsider changing his mind and join them as one family unit moving forward. This statement got an even louder banging on the table as everyone shouted, "hear! hear!" while looking over at Joe.

38

One year later in the upmarket area of Costa Adeje, South Tenerife, as Part Owner and Bar Manager of The Queen Vick 2, Sheila Callery looked around a packed house on opening night; she could feel the nervous excitement and butterflies in her tummy. She smiled across at Joe, their Back Stage Manager who was putting together the last few bits and pieces before the show started. He caught her eye looking at him and smiling back at her blew her a kiss. She then looked into the busy kitchen to see Neil the Executive Chef directing their staff with military precision; when he caught her eye, he smiled and gave her a wink. As she made her way back to the bar, Rose grabbed her from behind saying...

"Jesus Sheila, I think I'm going to have a fucking heart attack, I need a stiff drink".

Sheila smiled back saying, "Now Rose, as our dynamic Front of House Person and Compere, you have to stay sharp. But if you are a good girl, I'll have one waiting for you when you come off the stage", then taking a closer look at Rose, she said, "by the way, you look absolutely fabulous".

Rose kissed and hugged her before heading for the stage to introduce the first act of the night as she said...

"Wish me luck", and Sheila replied, "break a leg".

As Sheila watched her sister walking onto the stage, she beamed with pride to see how much she had changed; even after her baby girl Mary was born, she retained her beautiful figure. Frank was seated at a VIP table and had the buggy beside him; when people looked under the black-out cover to see the child, they laughed to see a beautiful little girl all dressed in pink fast asleep with a pink teddy beside her. But on her head she wore an industrial pair of ear muffs to keep out the noise of the show.

Seated beside him were the Dalton brothers and their wives who had travelled all the way from Muckalee in County Kilkenny Ireland. Also, there was Tommy and Vivienne Mc Cann who came to support them in their new venture. After the first act had finished, Rose walked out onto the stage again inviting the crowd to put their hands together in appreciation. Then slowly she built up her introduction for the main act of the night as if she had being doing it all her life, without a shred of nerves.

She began, "Ladies and Gentlemen", (and those of you who desire to transition), the one you have been waiting for, yes. It's the one and only, QUEEEEN VICK !!!"

The crowd went wild as Rose raised her arm and Bill Vickers swished onto the stage in a magnificent drag costume. As he broke into his opening number, Rose slipped away to join Sheila and Neil at the bar to watch the show.

The night was a total success; afterwards the party went on until the early hours of the morning with numerous bottles of champagne opened in celebration.

39

The next morning, Sheila woke to the sun shining through the blinds in their rented five bedroom villa a short stroll from the Queen Vick 2. She turned to see Conchita smiling back at her; they kissed on the lips then Sheila jumped out of bed to go and see if there was any coffee made. As she walked into the dining room, Joe was sitting at the table reading the morning paper; she ruffled his hair as she walked by. He told her there was fresh coffee in the pot and he had made croissants that were still in the oven. Through the French doors, Sheila could see Neil and Rose chatting and laughing in the swimming pool.

She enquired about Bill and Joe answered while shrugging his shoulders, "You know Bill, he likes his beauty sleep", as they both smiled in agreement. As she sat beside Joe at the table, they held hands in friendship, then Joe announced...

"Who would have thought!!!"

Sheila looked at Joe expectantly. Joe smiled at Sheila again and said, "Who would have thought that, if you had told me six months previously, I would be sitting here having resigned from my secure job in Ireland. Then to have my home upgraded and let out on Air B&B so I could pay my share of the rent on this fabulous house on this beautiful Island. And now to be working as a back stage manager in the Queen Vick 2, I would have had you committed into an institution for the bewildered". Joe stopped and thought for a minute, and then he said, "I wonder what my parents would think of me now?"

Sheila replied, "They would have been very proud of you for being so bold and taking such a big leap of faith in joining our team here". She continued, "And besides, we had to do a similar upgrade on our house and it is working out fine, and we have the option to go home if we like".

Nodding his head in agreement with Sheila, he said then...

"We would be lost without Bill, he has had some great ideas, and he knows how to put them into action".

Sheila answered, "He has indeed".

She got up from the table and walked out onto the patio to let the morning sun shine on her face and reflect on Joe's statement about Bill.

40

As she further reflected, she thought about the positive effect Bill had on her life, and as she looked around at her family together, she realized in fact it was all of their lives. She recalled the first time she met Bill in Cyprus and how much she disliked him for his negative attitude when they were introduced as Neil's daughters. She knew now that he wanted to say something but held back in fear of upsetting Neil. Then she thought of how she wanted to hit him when he burst in on them in the apartment just as her father was about to tell her why he had run away. Then Joe's statement came back into her head... "We would be lost without him".

The realisation of the statement dawned on her for the first time as she thought to herself.

"WHERE WOULD WE BE WITHOUT HIM/ HER?" As she now loved both of his personas.

She remembered her father saying, "Bill pleaded with me to make contact with the girls when they were in Cyprus".

But her father felt that they would be better off without him in their lives. Then she thought of what would have happened to Neil if Bill had not taken him in when his mind was in such a depressed state; God knows what he might have done to himself. And how Bill retired from the British Army to marry her dad so they could set up in business without any funding from Neil. This gave him back his self respect, independence, and above all, loving companionship.

As Sheila looked around, she could see her father and sister laughing in the pool, Joe was back reading his paper contentedly; Conchita, their Accountant/Payroll Manager who was the love of her life was lying in her bed upstairs. As the scales fell from her eyes, she then realised it was all Bill's foresight how they could come together as a dynamic family team and open the Queen Vick 2. Bill said how they could finance it through the short term let of the houses, Bill's and Neil's army pensions, as well as the built up money in Neil's accounts. And in Bill's own words, he said, as well as having a dynamic team, he then threw his hands in the air saying flamboyantly...

"Tra la, how could we fail darlings!!!"

Just then Bill strolled into the kitchen looking the worst for wear; he was unshaven, had bright red cheeks, and his hair was dishevelled. He slovenly threw himself into a soft chair and asked nobody in particular, "Was there any coffee in the pot?"

Sheila immediately got him some croissants and a big mug of coffee with milk and four spoons of sugar, just as he liked it. She put it down on the coffee table beside him. Then she went around behind his chair and kissed him tenderly on his bald patch. Bill acting all theatrically, but smiling at the same time, asked her, "What was that for darling?"

Sheila just smiled back and said, "That is just for being you, you gorgeous human being".

41

The Queen Vick 2 was a total success over the next four years; it went from strength to strength, but the hard work and late nights were beginning to take its toll on both Neil and Bill. It was Frank who noticed it first as he would only come over to Tenerife every quarter to inspect and sign off on the books. He made his concerns known to Rose and Sheila that he had seen a big deterioration in both men since his previous visit. Rose and Sheila hadn't really noticed as they were at home with them daily and also working hard with them nightly in the club. But they both decided they would keep a closer eye on them to make sure they were looking after themselves.

As Sheila watched them more closely, she was heartened to see them both in each other's company on their time off going shopping, or casually strolling hand in hand down the promenade in the sunshine. They would stop off at some coffee shop or other for cake, happily chatting to each other or the waiter who served them as they were well liked and respected business men in the community. She did notice however that they would sleep more and

Bill would go straight home to bed as soon as he came off stage instead of coming back into the club to mingle with the regular customers as he loved the buzz of talking to people after the show. Neil used to always stay back with the kitchen staff to make sure everything was ship-shape for the next day, but now she noticed he would leave with Bill as soon as he was ready. Sheila worried on how to approach the situation tactfully; she wanted to try and alleviate their workload and not cause offence to the two main patriarchs of the business whom she loved dearly. Unfortunately, as it happened, the opportunity presented itself soon afterwards. It was a weekend night and Bill had given one of the best performances of his career; the audience were delighted and as usual they were giving him a standing ovation calling him out again and again for an encore. Bill of course loved the applause and would sashay back on to the stage to take another bow. Just then, as Bill stepped forward to take his last bow, he suddenly fell forward onto the front four tables nearest the stage, knocking glasses and bottles flying. The customers scattered to try and save him from hitting the floor but they couldn't reach him quickly enough. In shock at what just happened, the whole club went quiet as Sheila ran from behind the bar. By the time she knelt beside Bill, Neil was by her side also holding his hand ashen faced. With a look of wide eyed disbelief on his face, Bill lay on the floor not knowing what had happened.

With tears running down his cheeks, Neil tried to comfort him saying, "Don't move my darling, you just had a slight fall which knocked the wind out of you. Just rest now for the moment and you will be fine again". Rose appeared with Joe and told Sheila that an ambulance was on its way. As it was the end of the night, they said they would also try and clear the audience, but while still standing and looking on in shock at what just happened, the regular customers were refusing to leave as they somehow felt compelled to stay and make sure that Bill was OK before they went home.

Within minutes which felt like hours, the First Responders arrived and knelt beside Bill. Sheila was surprised at their familiarity with Bill calling him by his name as they gave him oxygen and took his blood pressure. But one of the team glanced up at her smiling and said that he was a big fan of him/her, and Sheila felt better that he was being treated by a friend.

After taking Bill's readings, they looked concerned and said they would need to take him to hospital; they also knew Neil was his next of kin and said he too could accompany him. As Bill was lifted onto the gurney, Sheila looked at him so frightened like a little boy, and then at her father, white with fear walking beside him while still holding his hand; she thought her heart would break for the two of them. As the ambulance pulled away from the Queen Vick 2, a crowd had gathered around it; with its blue lights flashing and siren blaring, they seemed to form an opening on each side of the road to let it pass. Then to Sheila's delight, the crowd started to clap, cheer, and whistle as the ambulance passed them in honour of Bill. That night, Bill didn't make it to hospital; he just closed his eyes while holding Neil's hand and peacefully breathed his last breath as it was his time to go.

42

Rose and Joe said that they would lock up the club while Sheila raced to the hospital. When she entered the waiting area and saw her dad in floods of tears, she already knew the news was bad as she ran to his open arms to console him. While holding each other, Neil lifted his head and whispered in Sheila's ear that Bill had a premonition this was going to happen; also this was the way he wanted to go. He continued saying that when they were pulling away from the club and Bill heard the crowd cheering for him, he opened his eyes, squeezed Neil's hand, and while smiling, closed his eyes again for the last time. Sheila thought to herself that it was a lovely way to pass on but for now she knew Neil was devastated and hoped he could cope with the loss of his husband. Because of Bill's sudden death, a post mortem had to be conducted so his remains were brought to Santa Cruz after Neil signed all the official documentation. He also informed his only sister in England of his passing, but because she was also old and frail, she said she would not be able to attend his funeral. She sent Neil her sincere condolences on his great loss as Bill had told her how happy they had been together.

A verdict of natural causes was recorded for Bill's passing and his remains were released to Neil for cremation; it was a further three weeks before Bill's ashes came home to Neil. It gave them time to organise a nice send-off ceremony that they thought Bill would like, and it also kept Neil busy planning the details, but all the while Sheila worried for her father who she knew was broken hearted as she was for him.

It was decided that they would hold a humanist ceremony on Playa de Fanabe beach where Bill's ashes would be released into the Atlantic Ocean where he and Neil had strolled together hand in hand to watch the surfers while they had coffee and cake in the sunshine. It was also arranged that anyone who attended, could pick a restaurant of their choosing and have coffee and cake on the house, something that all proprietors agreed to happily.

On the morning of the ceremony, Sheila noticed that Neil hadn't come down for breakfast; she decided to check on him to see if he was alright. On entering the room, she could see her dad still in the bed and knew before she approached him that he had passed away peacefully in his sleep during the night. She sat beside his bed while taking his cold hand in hers and gently kissed him on the forehead while whispering in his ear for him to go and meet Bill, and not to worry, as she would take care of everything. She stayed with him a while longer while she wept for his passing before regaining her composure, then going back to the others to tell them the sad news.

Bill's ceremony was cancelled as word spread across a stunned congregation of Neil's passing but people spoke in hushed tones of how happy they were together and how nice that they were reunited again now. A further three weeks later Sheila, Rose, Frank, Joe, and little Mary stood knee deep in the water of Playa de Fanabe beach as they released the ashes of Neil and Bill Vickers/Callery into the Atlantic Ocean to a packed promenade of people clapping, cheering and whistling as they did so.

After a long sad day, the family were back in the house sitting around after dinner reminiscing about the events of Bill and Neil's passing. As it was getting late and it was bed time for little Mary, Sheila said that she would bring her up to bed. As she tucked the little girl in, Mary said to Sheila not to be sad about her dad. Sheila smiled at her saying that she was only a little sad and was happy for him also but would miss him. Then Mary said that if she missed him, all she had to do was go to sleep and he would visit her in her dreams as he did for her.

Sheila was a bit surprised at this statement and asked Mary did Neil visit her in her dreams?

Mary replied, "Oh yes and she would also see Uncle Bill and Nana Mary as well while she cycled her tricycle on the promenade; they would be drinking coffee together and they would wave at her happily as she passed".

This pleased Sheila as she kissed Mary and said, "Go to sleep now and dream those lovely dreams".

Later Sheila told Rose about the conversation she had with Mary about her dreams; Rose just smiled back at Sheila while winking at her saying, "She's a chip off the old block, our Mary", and Sheila remembered when Rose was in hospital saying that their mother used to visit her in her dreams, and wondered.

43

A week later Sheila and Rose returned to Stoneybatter, the next day was a cold and damp February morning. As arranged, their taxi pulled into the graveyard. They were heartened to see a guard of honour comprised of United Nations Veterans standing each side of their mother's grave and a lone piper standing at the head. As Sheila and Rose knelt over their mother's grave, with a small trowel they dug a hole and interred a small canister of their father's ashes. At the same time, the guard of honour lowered their flag as a mark of respect for their comrade while the piper played a lament, then the soldier's poem was read over the grave in a very solemn ceremony.

Afterwards the girls were invited back to the UN Headquarters Post 1 on Mount Temple road for refreshments and to meet with the veterans. It was a lovely afternoon and they thanked each veteran individually for their help and support before heading back to the airport.

After landing in Reina Sofia airport, they caught a bus for Costa Adeje bus terminal where Frank and Mary were waiting to pick them up. On the journey back, Sheila looked out the bus window at the snow-capped Mount

Teide Mountain and remembered back to the day she had decided to stay after getting a glimpse of her father.

She thought to herself, what would have happened if she had decided to board the plane with Joan that day, and where would her life be now? It seemed she had come full circle as she smiled to herself and felt the future looked bright with Conchita and her whole extended family going forward.

The End

Acknowledgements

Irish Defence Force Military Archives.
Irish United Nations Veterans Association, I.U.N.V.A.
Organisation of National Ex-Service Personnel, O.N.E.
To my fellow students of the IUNVA creative writing course, namely Sean Ryan. A resident of Stoneybatter who provided me with the photograph of Oxmanstown Road in the 1940s as a cover photo. And in particular, our tutor Ms Aoife Kerrigan, for her encouragement in early drafts of this book.
To my fellow comrades and U.N. Veterans, who served in UNFICYP, especially Ex Quartermasters Paul Cooley and Thomas Mc Cann with his wife Vivienne.
Private Chris Brennan of the Defence Forces Printing Press for his invaluable help in the design of the cover and contents of this book.
My niece Leah Hensey who kept me on the straight and narrow by proof reading my work.
My daughter Jenny who provided the limerick from her school days.
Finally, and most of all, my love and thanks to my wife Marian for all your patience, help, and advice in bringing this book forward.

I would sincerely like to express my gratitude to orla of Orla Kelly Publishing for being so pleasant and easy to work and to her designer Louise of 2funkidesign for giving me all your help to put a professional finish on my book.

Please Review

Dear Reader,

Thank you for taking the time to read my first novel. If you enjoyed it, I'd really appreciate if you'd tell others about it to help spread the word. And if you purchased it online, it would be great if you could post a review.

Thank you

Jimmy